A BERRY DEADLY
WELCOME

A.R. WINTERS

JOIN THE AR WINTERS NEWSLETTER!

Find out about the latest releases by AR Winters, and get access to exclusive free copies of her books:

Click Here To Join

You can also follow AR Winters on Facebook

∾

A Berry Deadly Welcome (A Laugh-Out-Loud Kylie Berry Mystery)

∾

When Kylie Berry moved to the small town of Camden Falls hoping for a fresh start, she never expected to be accused of murder.

But the despicable Rachel Summers is killed - apparently by Kylie's brownies!

Now it's up to Kylie to uncover the real murderer, all while dealing with the quirky inhabitants of the lovely town she's starting to call home.

CHAPTER 1

"*C*ome on, come on." I gripped the steering wheel with white knuckles. My car was out of gas. Rather, my ex-husband's car was out of gas. I had "borrowed" it to make the trip from Chicago, Illinois down to Camden Falls, Kentucky. I'd had to make the trip somehow, and I'd been too broke to buy a bus ticket.

I rocked back and forth in my seat a couple of times, trying to will my momentum into the car. I knew that wouldn't help it inch forward off the road and into the curbside parking spot, but I did it all the same. I couldn't stop myself.

"Just a little more!" The engine gagged, coughed, spluttered and then bucked before rattling and dying. That was okay, though.

When it bucked, the car lurched forward that little bit more that I'd needed to get it off the road. I wasn't going to have to abandon it with its butt end sticking halfway out into the road.

I eyed the road around me. It was huge. It wasn't eight lanes huge or anything like that. There were only two lanes, one coming and one going, but the main street of little Camden Falls could have accommodated four tractor trailers driving side by side. Even with so much room, the traffic was slow and lazy, cars meandering instead of rushing. There were two and three car-lengths between each car that passed. I was used to seeing cars in Chicago drive headlight to bumper, but that wasn't happening here.

On top of that, there were almost no people. I eyeballed around thirty or forty people walking around. They walked in small groups or alone, but always spread out with plenty of distance in-between.

I turned my attention toward a pickup truck that was driving past. The truck's driver nodded his head at me and then lifted his palm in a small side-to-side wave. Panic flooded me, and my heart skittered and jumped as badly as the engine had a moment earlier. My ex probably already had a warrant out for my arrest, and it would be just like him to hire someone to keep an eye out for me.

I twisted to see if anything was coming from behind and then jumped out of the car. It was a pearl white Mercedes S-Class, and I'd probably never get the chance to drive anything like it again—especially if my ex had me put in jail. If that happened, I wouldn't even need to worry about how I'd look when I renewed my driver's license. I wouldn't need to worry about where my next meal was coming from or where I was going to sleep tonight.

"Maybe I should get arrested." I couldn't keep the hopefulness out of my voice as I glanced around, but I didn't see any police. "Live to fight another day," I said with a scowl before forcing my features to relax. I didn't want to get wrinkles.

Popping the trunk of the car, I used all of my not-impressive strength to lift a navy canvas suitcase out of the trunk. Then, I hesitated, looking wistfully between the car keys I held in my hands and the car. With a sigh and a shoulder shrug, I did what I had to do. I clicked the lock button on the key fob, and then tossed the keys into the trunk and slammed the trunk's lid down. I'd gotten this far, but tempting fate wasn't my style.

I pulled up the suitcase's telescoping handle and started walking, dragging the suitcase behind me on its tiny wheels. The name tag attached to the handle flopped and jiggled as I walked, listing my name in block letters: KYLIE BERRY. It was my maiden name, not the name I'd left behind with that dirty, rotten piece of pond scum I used to call a husband. No, Kylie Berry was a good name, and it, the suitcase and its contents were all that I owned. But that would be enough. It had to be. I'd figure out the rest as I went, and where I was going now was my cousin's cute little café. When she'd invited me to come down to "help her out," I'd jumped at it. If it meant one less night of having to sleep at the women's shelter, then I was game.

I paid attention to the people around me as I walked. All around me were a myriad of tennis shoes or flat sandals, various types of denim, a few Walmart-style short skirts, and a lot of t-shirts. I was wearing a black polka-dotted sleeveless, torso-fitted dress with a flared skirt, gold high-heel pumps, and I knew from experience that my shoulder-blade length fire red hair would be shining in the afternoon sun.

4

I didn't fit in, but I didn't see anyone picking up any rocks to throw at me, so I figured that must be okay. A man exited a store with a green awning twenty or so feet ahead of me wearing what had to have been a thousand-dollar suit, and no one paid him any attention either.

"Things are going to be okay," I mumbled to myself. Yet my feet were not convinced. Camden Falls' Main Street seemed to go on forever, and my pretty gold pumps soon pinched my feet in ways that made me work hard to hide a limp.

A group of barely twenty-somethings sauntered through a door a little ways ahead of me laughing, and one of them was holding a to-go cup of what looked like iced tea.

My heart sped up but my feet slowed. This was it. My new beginning. My second chance. I'd be the best waitress, assistant, whatever I could be to Sarah. And hopefully, Sarah would make room for me on her couch until I crawled my way back up to standing on my own two feet.

This would work. I would *make it* work.

CHAPTER 2

I won't lie, when I reached for the glass-front door with the scrawling script "Sarah's Eatery" on it, my hand was shaking, but I kept my eyes bright and an excited smile on my gloss-painted lips as I pulled the door open. A little bell jangled, announcing my entrance.

That's when I stepped into cousin Sarah's "tiny" little café, and my smile slipped as my mouth fell open. It was huge! I had imagined some ten foot by ten foot space with as many little round tables and chairs as could be crammed into it per the laws of physics, but instead what I found was spatial extravagance. There was room to walk between the tables.

People could have conversations without the absolute certainty that the words they spoke were being overheard by the person sitting two inches behind them. A ladder on top of another ladder would be needed to reach the ceiling. And it had big, sunny windows on two sides, all along the wall that faced Main Street and all along the wall that faced the corner side street, making it look even bigger.

"Wow." I felt like I was Dorothy in *The Wizard of Oz*. I'd been swept up from the churning bustle of Chicago and dropped right in the middle of a magical place where people could stretch their legs, lean back in their chairs and prop their arms behind their heads without worrying about blocking the path of another.

"Kylie!" Sarah exclaimed.

I turned my head to the left, toward Sarah's voice and a grill-style bar. Over the bar was a large banner that read, "We'll miss you!" with Sarah's name taped on at the end on a large piece of colorful construction paper. Sarah had her hands thrown up in the air as if to celebrate, and all of the patrons at the bar were swiveled around on their stools to stare at me.

Sarah didn't exactly come running from around the bar to greet me. It's more like she bounced. She was wearing denim overalls that were rolled at the ankle, a sleeveless tee with a scoop neck, and cute little white canvas shoes without socks. Her eyes crinkled heavily at the corners from her enormous smile, but it looked good on her.

"Hey!" She threw her arms around me in a warm, snuggly hug. Her hair smelled like apples with a hint of grilled cheese. "I knew you'd make it in time."

"Hi," I said, with a panic-smile plastered on my face. "You going somewhere?"

Sarah sighed and got dreamy-eyed. "I just couldn't wait a minute more to go join Jon in Seattle. All my stuff is packed and ready to go."

Breathe. Keep breathing, I told myself while another little voice inside my head screeched, *Homeless! You're going to be sleeping on the streets!*

I should have kept the car keys. I could have at least slept in it. A crowbar. I could break into the trunk in the middle of the night. And the trunk was roomy! No one would have to see me sleeping in the car. I could use the clothes in my suitcase to make a cozy little bed for myself.

"That's great." My voice barely wavered, but I felt a cold sweat breaking out on my upper lip.

"Come on," she said, grabbing my hand and

pulling me along behind her. "I want you to meet the regulars. This going away party was their idea."

I eyed them, wondering if one of them would take over the café. Then I wondered if they would give me a job. Back in Chicago, I had transformed my ex-husband's heating and air installation and repair shop from a business that was barely making it into one that was thriving. We had even expanded to take on complex HVAC installation and repair for large building complexes. I'd secured service contracts with three different hospitals that brought in hundreds of thousands of dollars. But when we split up, he poisoned every well of goodwill I had built for myself. None of our friends would take my calls, and I suspected that he'd even bribed a cop to falsify my information with a police record so that I couldn't pass background checks. I hadn't been able to get a job anywhere with anyone. Almost overnight, I'd become an outcast and a penniless leper.

I made him, and he ruined me.

"Hi!" I said with the biggest, brightest smile I could muster. I lifted my hand to wave a greeting, but it was trembling worse than when

I'd opened the door of the cafe and I quickly dropped it back down to the side of my thigh.

Whoever these people were sitting in front of me, I needed them. I didn't know why yet, but I knew that my future depended on them. Nobody liked the stink of desperation, though, so I had to keep my situation to myself.

"This is Jack, Brad, Joel, Agatha and Zoey," Sarah said as she did a Vanna White and pointed to each one with an extended arm as she called out their names. There was a murmured chorus of friendly but subdued hellos.

I did a quick analysis of each. Jack was a tall, fit, forty-something businessman in a nice suit with shiny, immaculate, stylish, expensive-looking leather shoes. His skin was the color of hot cocoa, and he was definitely the frontrunner in my guess of who was the café's new owner.

Next to Jack was Brad. Handsome, handsome, handsome Brad. I had to force myself not to stare at him, or lean into him, or tell him that I wanted to have his babies. Brad had baby blue eyes that looked as though they could have a woman undressing before she ever realized what her traitorous hands were doing. Yet when he smiled, leaned forward and extended his hand to shake, all I saw in his face was a sweet boy who was happy to meet his friend's cousin. But that beguiling boyish face of his was tempered into something much more imposing because of the law enforcement uniform he was wearing. On his shoulder was a black, gold, and white patch that said, "Kentucky State Police."

I was sure that the sweat on my upper lip grew even worse when I shook his hand.

Next to Brad was Joel. He raised the palm of his dinner-plate-sized hand in greeting and said, "Hi," while wearing a big smile that I could only describe as that of a sexy goofball. And, the way he said even the word "hi" with a thick accent, making it sound as if it was two syllables instead of one because of a brief E sound that he added to the end. He was dressed in a flannel shirt over top a white t-shirt and khaki pants. There was a gentleness in his eyes and in his way of being that soothed my nerves and lulled me into the sense that everything was going to be okay, yet his powerful physique was that of someone who was driven and passionate about life, someone who liked to win. I got the impression that coming in second place would never be good enough for that man.

Next to Joel was Agatha, a woman who maybe weighed 110 pounds if her pixie-cut white hair was sopping wet. The cascade of necklaces, earrings, and bracelets the octogenarian wore could have added a few extra pounds, though. Her dress was free-flowing yet elegant, and though she wasn't wearing East Indian attire, I got the impression that she would have been able to walk down any street in Kolkata with the air of an ancient and powerful goddess. Her small, dark, wise eyes edged on beady, but their small size seemed to concentrate the strength with which she could look inside my soul.

I swallowed when I shook her hand, and hoped that I would be able to keep my humiliating circumstances to myself, but I felt as though she already knew them and had accepted them without judgment.

Finally, there was Zoey, a young Asian woman with flawless honey skin who looked to be somewhere between twelve and thirty years of age. She was fearlessly dressed in skin-tight olive green jeans that had designer thread-bare holes up one thigh and the opposite knee torn out. Her midriff-exposing sleeveless, high-necked, white top hugged her every curve, and her black eyeliner was nothing short of fierce. But she looked like she was about to cry and her full lips were pinched together as if to stop a tremble.

These people loved Sarah. I'd be nothing more than day-old leftovers once she was gone. When I left Chicago, I'd thought I was running to something. My bleak days had gained new hope. But I was no better off today than I was yesterday or the day before... or any day before for the last three months.

"Come on. I've got the papers in the back," Sarah said, grabbing my hand and pulling me along behind her. We rounded the corner of the grill-bar and then stepped through to a kitchen that was all stainless steel and industrial. Even the countertops were stainless steel. The place was spotless.

Stopping abruptly, she parked us in front of a thin stack of papers.

"I had my lawyer draw these up, and he said that everything in them was beyond fair and reasonable." She flipped through the papers. "You won't need to start paying me back until you either start showing a profit or three years have passed. There's no interest attached to the equity, and we can set up a payment plan based on your profit margin." She flipped to the last page and pointed to an empty signature slot next to a line that already bore her name. "This is where you sign."

I flipped back to the front page. It read, "Purchase of Business Agreement." I was so stunned that I forgot to breathe until the room began to shift gently on its axis. I then gulped air like I'd been under water for ages. "You're selling me the café?"

CHAPTER 3

"Yeah, silly," Sarah said, concern creeping into her voice as she looked at me with confusion in her eyes. "I sent emails with all the details."

I hadn't gotten emails and my smartphone had gotten turned off a month and a half ago because I hadn't been able to pay the bill. I'd talked to Sarah twice in hurried calls on a "borrowed" phone before sneaking it back into my women's shelter roommate's bag. Now some of the things Sarah had said as I'd listened with one ear to her and the other listening for the return of my roommate made sense.

"You're selling me the café," I said again, this time with wonder in my voice as my gaze traveled to take in all that was around me. Tinker Bell must have sprinkled fairy dust on everything in those moments before my synapses connected with what was happening, because now everything sparkled. I was sure that it wasn't because of the tears gathering in my eyes.

A clang sounded from the back corner of the kitchen and I peered around hanging pots and pans to see a short Italian-looking man with thick black hair beating a bowl of something pale, semi-wet and semi-firm. I didn't have a clue what it could be, and that's when it struck me. I didn't know a thing about cooking!

"That's Roberto," Sarah whispered as she handed me a pen. "I'd have been lost without him. His food is amazing!"

I took the pen, bent over the contract and signed it without reading it. The last time I'd done that was when I was eighteen and my twenty-seven-year-old fiancé put a prenup in front of my face and then made me feel rude and unloving when I wanted to read it before signing it. I hadn't read it then and I wasn't reading it now, but this time it because I was afraid that if I took the time to look the contract over, Sarah would realize what a mistake she was making and would take it all back.

Sarah whipped out her cell phone, lined all the pages up in a row and then took a picture of the whole thing. "You keep the originals and send me a copy when you get the chance. I want to finish showing you around before I hit the road."

My heart did an unsteady tap dance and I did my best not to hyperventilate. I gathered the papers in my hand and rolled them up, determined to keep them with me so that all of this didn't evaporate into thin air as easily as it had materialized.

Next, Sarah introduced me to Roberto, but he grunted and turned his back to me while continuing on with his work. He reminded me of an artist—complete with an artist's temperament.

Walking through the kitchen, she named off each of the major pieces of equipment before leading me into first the walk-in refrigerator and then the walk-in freezer. Both looked fairly well stocked, but I had no concept of how long food would last in a restaurant. I knew what I was seeing was all that I'd have to work with. I didn't have any money for buying more supplies, unless I "borrowed" from the cash transactions to cover some expenses.

A flash of fear shot through me. Roberto got a paycheck, surely. So did the few waiters and waitresses who I'd seen drifting around the dining area when I came in. I'd have nothing to pay them with!

Heading out of the kitchen, Sarah showed me around the rest of the place. She demonstrated how the register worked and introduced me to the staff. Meanwhile, I kept my eyes open for a spot where I could curl up and sleep tonight. I wasn't going to have to break into the car after all. And the temperature-controlled café would provide me a lot more comfort against the now-chill autumn nights.

Everything Sarah showed me flew by me, and I caught and retained what tidbits I could attach to my still-stunned brain. She must have seen my effort to take everything in because she laid her delicate fingered hand on my arm, winked and reassured me, "We can Skype anytime you need to talk."

I nodded with a smile and then added buying a laptop to my list of things to do ASAP.

I didn't notice the keys she put in my hand until she curled my fingers around them. "It's all yours now," she said as a tear slid down her cheek, and I felt as though I finally had a free pass to let some tears fall myself.

I don't know who hugged who first, but we wrapped each other up in our arms. When we pulled away, she held my hand that had the keys. There were two of them.

"This one is to the front and back doors of the café," she said, "and this one is to the apartment upstairs. I didn't have any need for my mattress, so I left it for you."

I squeaked. I hadn't even realized that my mouth was open, but I squeaked all the same. Recovering as best I could, I said, "Thanks." It came out as a breathy whisper. It was the best I could do, except that I gathered her in for another hug.

True to Sarah's word, she really was packed and ready to go. I stood in the open back door of the café and waved as she drove her U-Haul truck out of the café's back parking lot.

Turning back around, my eyes scanned the building that I now owned. *That I own...* Glee, fear, and unbridled excitement battled inside of me, but I smiled from ear to ear like the lucky fool that I was.

I was home.

CHAPTER 4

*F*or the rest of the day, I took turns following around various wait staff and chef, Roberto. I was pretty sure that I was annoying the heck out of all of them, except for one kid who kept acting super guilty about something. He kept giving me worried glances over his shoulder and looking at me like I was a narc. I tried to tell him that I was just trying to learn from him, but after he'd stammered and sweated his way through his third table of customers, I let the poor boy be and went to shadow Roberto in the kitchen.

But following Roberto around in the kitchen made *me* sweat. He didn't shoot me worried, guilty looks. He shot me dirty, angry looks. He finally left off making a delicious looking Waldorf salad and instead stood in front of me while he sharpened his knives on a long, tapered, round rod. He looked at me the whole time like he was either going to stab me or spear me.

That's when I graciously left him to his work. I had to go all the way outside the café to find out what time the café closed. The café's front door said that it opened at 7:30 AM and closed at 10 PM, Monday through Saturday. On Sunday, it opened at 10 AM and closed at 4 PM.

"Holy smokes," I said. My body was vibrating with fatigue. I'd already driven seven hours non-stop from Chicago to Camden Falls. I wasn't sure I could survive another five hours before finally being able to collapse in my as-of-yet mysteriously located apartment. I had no idea how Sarah managed a restaurant that was open for fourteen and a half hours a day.

I stepped out of the way while one of the waitresses came through the door. Her name tag said Melanie. She had her purse slung over her shoulder, and a cute little half-apron still tied around her waist. Her shoulder-length hair was reddish-brown with curls that could have made Shirley Temple a tad bit jealous. They framed her heart-shaped face beautifully.

"Goodnight," she said, giving me a pleasant smile while all I could think was, *Of course she's smiling! She's off of work! I'll never be off of work again in my life!* I didn't know much about running an eatery but I knew enough to know that the work didn't begin and end with your first and last customer. No, there were numbers to tally. I didn't know what numbers or for what purposes, but I knew that they were there and I was pretty sure that I was the one who had to count them.

There were people to pay, inventory to take, and salt shakers to refill.

"Goodnight," I said, parroting Melanie. As she turned to walk away, she untied her apron and then draped it over her arm.

That's it! I'm the boss! The words rang like the Hallelujah chorus. *I'm the boss!*

I stepped back inside the café and looked all around me at the wonderful, beautiful, amazing people that Sarah had trained. I didn't have to do everything. No, I got to tell other people what to do.

My smile grew and grew until my cheeks hurt.

"Sam," I said, snagging a young waiter as he headed back to the kitchen with an empty tray. He was tall and lanky with thick black hair that seemed to want to grow taller rather than longer. He was somewhere between nerdy cute and athletic cute. "Can you tell me who... um..." I didn't know the words. "Who wraps things up for the night?"

"Amy and Paul are scheduled to close tonight."

Another beautiful word. Scheduled! "Where can I find the schedule?"

Sam pulled his cell phone from his back pocket, thumbed through whatever screens he needed to navigate and then handed the device over to me. "Sarah always sends everyone an email with the schedule for the week."

I gulped. Email. There was an excellent chance that I was going to have to go old-school on everyone with some paper and pens.

The look on my face must have been price-less because Sam took pity on me. "We've got this down here if you want to head up to your apartment. Sarah usually used the slow hours to take care of management stuff and then would head upstairs after the dinner rush, but everyone would understand if you needed to take off early." I was torn between throwing my arms around him in a hug or planting a big, inappropriate kiss right on his lips. Either way, he took my silence as an opportunity to keep on talking, and that was just fine by me. "Brenda will be in early in the morning to take care of setup."

"Sam, you've been great. Remind me to give you a raise when I can afford to give you one." For some reason that made him blush and smile as he dropped his eyes bashfully. "I've got just one other question for you. How do I get up to the apartment?"

~

The answer had been a door at the back of the kitchen, and now I stood at the top of an L-shaped flight of stairs in front of a heavy wooden door that had been painted canary yellow. The stairwell was full of shadows, but the door was so bright that I felt safe captured within its haloed reflection.

I fumbled with the first key and then the second, trying to figure out which one fit the latch. I finally got it right, turned the handle of the door and then stepped in.

I gasped. The apartment was enormous. No, no... that wasn't right. It was gigantic! I don't know why but I had imagined a tiny one-bedroom apartment with a kitchenette barely big enough to turn around in. Instead, I was looking at a space that was every bit as large as the café beneath me.

And it was empty.

I leaned in, certain that I had to be in the wrong place. One person couldn't have all of this space to themselves, and I was expecting a family of eight to materialize out of the walls demanding to know why I was in their home. But no one materialized and I instead closed the door behind me with a solid click, followed by the sound of me throwing the latch.

The floors were hardwood, the ceiling needed a ladder and a half to be reached, and all of the outer walls were the same red bricks as the outside of the building.

Dragging my little suitcase behind me, I gave myself a tour. The living room with windows overlooking Main Street was big enough to learn how to rollerblade in. There was a chef's kitchen decked out with a six-burner gas stove, two wall-insert ovens, and enough granite counter space to leave a quarry looking depleted. The middle island was big enough to double as a bed.

Feeling incredibly intimidated, I left the kitchen behind me to explore the rest of apartment. There was a bedroom, a guest bedroom, a bathroom that was the picture of simple elegance, and a smaller room that looked as though it had been used as an office.

True to Sarah's word, she had left me a mattress as well as a shower curtain. Beyond that, I found a couple of pans in the back of a cabinet in the kitchen, the pantry looked as though it were half-stocked with a variety of options ranging from canned soup to dried lentils, and the refrigerator had some eggs, milk, and some other items plus a pretty good selection in the freezer. On top of all of that, I'd found some abandoned coat hangers in one of the closets.

I was good. No, I was more than good. I was fine. Being good comes and goes, but being fine, that meant you had a roof over your head and the certainty of food in your belly.

I was fine, and I had truly never been happier than in that moment. For the first time in my life, I had freedom-plus, as in I could do what I wanted to do without a husband or even parents to tell me what to do, *plus* I had a means of supporting myself in that freedom.

Jumping up to sit on the kitchen counter to eat a popsicle from the freezer, I heard a crinkling and remembered the contract that I'd shoved down the front of my dress. Squirming a little in order to reach it, I pulled it out and started ready. I got two-thirds the way down the second page when I choked on my popsicle. "Two point five million!"

I felt a little faint as I scanned the rest of the pages, but on the second to the last page, I froze. It was a list of the acquisitions.

"I own the whole building," I whispered in disbelief, as in from one side street to the other. I owned the whole building, and included in the breakdown was a listing of the current rent being paid by each business in my building. It wasn't enough to pay off two and a half million dollars in a month, but it was enough to go buy myself a laptop and then some... as soon as they paid their rent.

Suddenly, my definition of the word "fine" changed a little, and I let some of that "good" creep into its meaning. Yes, I was going to be good *and* fine.

CHAPTER 5

I got up the next morning, took a shower without any shampoo or soap, and then walked around the apartment for half an hour naked to air dry since I didn't have any towels. It wasn't so bad. The shower was fast and walking around without any clothes on in a building that I owned felt empowering. I mean, what says ownership more than being able to walk around naked?

Next, I picked out clothes to wear. I figured I wouldn't be doing much of the manual labor since I had so many people working for me, but I wanted to fit in. I wanted my customers and staff to feel comfortable approaching me. So, I pulled on a pair of jeans that fit like leggings and a loose lavender tunic top.

I had no idea what time Brenda, the opener Sam had mentioned, got into work, but it was already 7:15 AM and the restaurant opened in another fifteen minutes. I wanted to get the chance to meet Brenda before the doors officially opened, and I thought me being up and present when the place opened would look good. Participating owner and all that.

Owner. The word still made me smile like a lunatic from ear to ear.

When I reached the bottom of the stairs and got to the door that would lead into the restaurant, I resisted the urge to knock first and tentatively stick my head in. I did feel as though I was walking into somebody else's space, but I needed to work past that. Perception was ninety-nine percent of what it took to succeed, and the people who worked for me needed me to act like their leader and not just be the person who signed their paychecks.

I really had to figure out how to do paychecks. I really had to figure out where to get the money for paychecks!

I needed to set up a bank account for cash deposits. I could stash the cash the apartment for now, but I didn't want to invite the possibility of someone breaking in in the middle of the night and, well... I refused to finish the thought.

This is Kentucky, I reminded myself. I'm not in Chicago. Fewer people. Fewer crimes. Made sense to me.

I compromised between opening the kitchen door and barging in and knocking first by opening it halfway and giving a tap on the door. I heard a low, pleasant humming of some song that was familiar but which I couldn't put a finger on.

"Hello?" I called out.

"Hello!" A slightly pudgy woman about five feet two inches with jet black hair appeared from around the corner. Spotting me, she made a bee-line right for me with her arms up in the air until she was able to wrap them around me. She tottered us from side to side, humming her pleasure. Pulling away, then, she held me captive but at arm's length. "Sarah told me so much about you," she said, beaming.

I wasn't sure that was a good thing or a bad thing, but I was going to go with good.

"That rotten husband of yours."

Definitely good... She was scowling and

pursing her lips so hard that I thought she might spit. My ex-husband seemed to have left as bad a taste in her mouth as he had in mine.

"Thank you. That's very nice of you to say."

"I've got brothers. I wish you had brothers. That man needed to be visited by a whole gang of brothers."

I couldn't keep the smile away from my face. "Thank you," I said again, and I'd never meant the words more.

Brenda's eyes narrowed and her lips pursed even more as her head started bobbing up and down to some thought she had in her head. "Honey, I got a text from Roberto. He quit."

My voice dropped two octaves. "He what?"

"He up and quit." She patted my shoulder in condolence. Then, releasing me, she walked away to return to her work of chopping vegetables and dropping them into a large pot of water to make what I assumed would be vegetable soup. "And I gotta leave early today. My grandson needs me to take him to the doctor this morning."

Grandson. Brenda looked to me to be in her early 40s. I was almost thirty with no kids, so her having a grandchild already kind of threw me for a loop.

"Okay," I said, trying to force my brain out of deer-in-headlights mode and into get-things-done mode. Problem was, I didn't know what I was supposed to get going.

"Now, you set this pot to simmering by ten o'clock and it will be ready to serve by eleven."

Fear gripped me. She was expecting me to cook. I knew what she was asking was for me to just turn the stove on and that she'd done all the prep work, but I still struggled to wrap my brain around it. "Okay," I said, nodding.

"Throw some salt and herbs in there, too, to flavor it up a bit." Brenda was taking off her apron. Brenda was getting ready to leave.

I nodded that I would do just as she'd told me. My brain screamed for me to ask what herbs I should use but my pride had super glued my mouth shut.

"Thanks, Brenda!" I called after her as she disappeared from the kitchen, finally finding my voice. I heard the café's front door chime as she made her escape.

I looked at a clock on the wall. 7:25 AM. I had a café to open. On my own.

"Oh snap."

CHAPTER 6

*L*unch time had started and I was whipping up anything that I thought I had an inkling of how to make. Only two wait staff had shown up, and one of them left forty-five minutes in without saying a word, leaving Sam to run around at a near constant jog in an attempt to take care of everybody. Thankfully his legs were long and he covered a lot of ground with every stride. He wasn't even breathing heavily.

He was definitely getting a raise—just as soon as I figured out how to pay people.

I was in the kitchen frantically stirring mayonnaise into chopped eggs to make egg salad. It was a little runny-looking to me, but eggs firmed things up, right? So, if I let it rest a few minutes, it would be more than fine. The yolks had turned out covered in green, but I figured that had something to do with hens that were out in the country instead of in the city.

Moving as fast as I could, I tore open a hoagie bun with my fingers and ladled an inch and a half's worth of egg salad onto it. I plopped that down on a plate and poured out a generous portion of potato chips from a bag I'd gotten out of Sarah's--I mean my--pantry. I then filled a bowl with Brenda's soup. I'd put the heat so high that it had ended up boiling for more than half an hour, so the vegetables were a little pale and mushy, but I was sure the flavor was fine.

Wearing a big, overly eager smile, I rushed the food out to where the customer was sitting at the grill bar. Wiping my hands on my food-stained apron, I waited with high anticipation for him to take a bite.

Eyeing me with what looked like a mixture of annoyance and uncertainty, he picked up the hoagie and took a big bite. All of the egg salad poured out the bun's butt end and sloshed all over the potato chips. With his mouth still stuffed with egg-less bread, the customer picked up a potato chip, and I watch in mortification as the chip slowly drooped, completely soggy.

Without saying a word, he slid off the bar stool, threw down a single dollar bill, and walked out.

I watched him go, then I said a bad word. I won't say which one, but Jack heard it and he chuckled. He was wearing another expensive-looking suit. His mocha-colored skin was stubble-free and his dark eyes laughed with amusement.

"You've been shoved right into the deep end of the pool," he said. He shook his head. "If only you could swim." A bowl of vegetable soup was sitting in front of him. It had been for fifteen minutes, but it didn't look as though it was any more empty than the moment I'd put it in front of him.

I darted forward. "I need a life preserver. I need a new chef. Roberto quit."

With his chin down, he looked at me from under his brows. "Your ex in-laws live around these parts, don't they." It came out as a statement instead of a question.

I nodded. Small as it is, it was a big enough town. There were other places for them to eat. I figured we'd be civil about it and simply avoid each other like every other well-adjusted adult.

"Last night was Wednesday." He didn't say any more, yet he looked at me as if he'd said a lot.

I was lost. "Um, and today's Thursday..." I really wasn't trying to be cheeky or anything. I simply wasn't connecting the dots he was seeing in his own head.

"Is your aunt-in-law Dorothy Hibbert?"

"My ex-aunt-in-law," I said, filled with trepidation as to where this was going.

"My cousin told me she was at church service last night, and she had a whooole lot to say about you."

Oh no.

"But the biggest thing she stressed was that you were bad—a bad wife, a bad influence, and a bad person. The way I heard it she all but claimed you were a witch and that no food you made should be trusted."

"I didn't make the soup," I blurted. I wasn't sure why I said it, but I knew I didn't want Jack to leave. I needed a friend, and seemed to me that he was trying to be a friend.

He smiled but was polite enough not to say anything about it, but he did continue on with his story. "She told everybody that they shouldn't eat here, they shouldn't work here, and that if they knew somebody that did work here that they would be doing God's work to make them quit.

My mouth fell open. "That b—" I stopped myself at b.

"Mmhmm," Jack agreed with me. "I think you're going to have trouble finding another chef. Roberto used to date Dorothy and I heard he's still carrying a torch for her. Between the two of them..."

I filled in the rest. I was up a creek without a paddle in sight. My eyes tracked Sam jogging past on his way to get someone a refill on their drink. My only wait staff here today. I was starting to understand. Not only had my ex tried to destroy me, but now his family was going to take their turn.

CHAPTER 7

I had survived another day of ownership of Sarah's Eatery, and with the chime of the kitchen stove's timer to wake me up, I was staring down the barrel of my third day. My body ached and my feet throbbed. I wanted to cry. As the day had moved into evening and I'd been the only person there to cook and serve people, customer after customer had gotten up and walked out. I'd lost count after number twenty-two. Finally, a group of high school-aged kids had come in laughing and looking at me as if I was some walking joke. It didn't take me long to figure out that they'd heard from someone how bad things had gotten at the café and had come down for the show. I think that one of the snot-nosed jerks had even recorded me on his smartphone.

Groaning, I rolled myself off of my sheetless mattress and onto the floor before pushing up to a standing position. I showered slower. I dressed slower. And when I went downstairs, I trudged into the kitchen with as much energy as a toddler six hours past nap time.

"Good morning!" It was Brenda's blessed voice. I stifled a sob, so happy that she hadn't abandoned me too.

"Brenda, how late can you work today?"

She sucked in a breath about the same as someone might if you asked them if they could jump the distance between two sides of a volcano.

"Mmmm, I think I could stay as late as 10:15 this morning."

"Is there anything you could make that I could... uh, heat up in the microwave when it was time to serve it?"

Her eyes studied her eyebrows from one side to the other while she contemplated my question. "Spaghetti," she finally said with a curt nod.

"Could you make—" I didn't know how

much to ask for. "Could you make enough to feed people for the rest of the day?"

"Oh! Hmmm, enough for three-hundred and fifty to five-hundred servings..."

I almost choked at her estimate. I was lucky if I'd had fifty paying customers yesterday, but I guess that spread over fifteen hours of service, that many meals wasn't that much. "You think you could make enough for, uh... a hundred?" I'd err on the side of optimism. People would eat Brenda's spaghetti, the day would go a lot smoother, and I'd have twice as many paying customers!

"Sure! I can do that." Brenda beamed.

This morning it was me throwing my arms around Brenda to give her a huge hug. She took it in stride, giving me a warm hug right back.

But luck was not with me, at least not that morning. From the time that we opened to the time that Brenda left at 10:15, the only customer who came in was Zoey. I tried to make her coffee—twice—but on the third attempt she came around to my side of the grill bar's counter and brewed it herself.

On the counter, she had a couple of books. One was *How to Know if He's a Jerk*, and the other was *How to Move on After Being Ghosted*.

Just like on the day Sarah left, Zoey looked as though she were on the verge of tears, and I realized that maybe it wasn't Sarah leaving that had made her so sad after all. For some odd, perverse reason, that made me happy. Somewhere inside my twisted brain, her not being so completely torn up by Sarah leaving meant that maybe she had room within her to like me.

We sat together in silence as she read her books and I studied Sarah's Eatery's menu. This was the first time I'd really sat down and looked at it. If I were going into a restaurant to order food, I would have felt completely comfortable and confident about what each dish was, but at being faced with having to make each dish, I was completely lost.

At 11 AM, Sam showed up, and as he'd promised me before taking off from work yesterday, he brought in his laptop so that I could use it to post an online ad for a new chef. Seven or eight people trickled in and out over the lunch rush, and Sam heated up the spaghetti in the microwave himself, his tall, lanky form moving from place to place silently and efficiently. I was thrilled when someone asked for a piece of cake until I realized we didn't have any to serve them.

In between serving the customers, Sam helped me set up an ad on Craigslist and on some local online classifieds. The allowed word count on some of the sites was limited, so we kept it short on all of them.

*W*anted: Chef
Experience and passion required.

Attention to detail.

Attention to excellence.

Available for long shifts.

Start Date: Immediate.

*W*e listed the café's phone number.

Again, as soon as possible, Sam was getting a raise.

When the lunch "rush" had ended and the afternoon slump had become a thing of the past, I drifted into an evening of absolutely no customers.

I checked how much spaghetti was left, and it was enough to drown myself in if I chose to. Instead, though, I filled up a huge bowl, locked the café's front door three hours early, turned off the café lights to show that we were closed, and I headed upstairs to my apartment.

Tonight I was a different kind of tired. My feet didn't ache, but fatigue had settled into my bones. I felt soul tired. I felt like maybe life had finally won, and I should just give up.

I searched the pantry until I found a bottle of wine. One way or another, I was going to sleep well tonight.

~

I woke up with a headache.

Okay, so maybe I woke up with a hangover, but I marched my way into the same routine. Shower. Dress. Head downstairs to meet Brenda.

No Brenda.

"No!" I stamped my foot, then I took a deep breath. "Okay, don't freak out. Maybe she takes weekends off."

I got to work. There was still plenty of pasta and spaghetti sauce that I could throw on a plate and heat up in a microwave. In fact, I fixed myself a plate and had it for breakfast before throwing myself into making a cake from scratch. I don't know why, but it had been downright embarrassing when the lunch customer yesterday had asked for cake and I hadn't had any to give him. So, I'd make a cake. I knew it couldn't be that hard. Some flour. Some eggs. Milk. Maybe even some chocolate chips. Who didn't like chocolate chips?

I fantasized about the customers giving me a standing ovation, whistling and hollering in celebration of my cake.

I just hadn't found the thing I was good at yet. That was all. And for all I knew, this cake could become my masterpiece...

It turned out hard enough and flat enough that it could have been used in a discus throw.

So, maybe cakes weren't my thing. That was okay. I'd keep looking.

"I'm here!" I heard someone call out and rushed out of the kitchen just in time to see Melanie rushing to put on her apron. Her reddish-brown hair fell in large curls around her heart-shaped face. "I'm sorry I'm late."

It was 11 AM. I hadn't had a customer all day, but Melanie showing up made me happier than a party of ten walking in through the door.

"You didn't quit!"

Melanie's face registered shock. "No, ma'am. I'm sorry I'm late. Please don't fire me."

A nervous giggled snuck its way out of me at the absurdity of me firing one of my last two wait staff. "I hadn't seen you in a couple of days. I thought maybe you'd quit."

"But I wasn't scheduled until today." She sounded scared, as though still worried that I would fire her.

"How late are you scheduled to work to today?"

"Five."

"Want to work 'til closing?"

Her face lit up. "Sure! I could use the extra hours."

"You scheduled for tomorrow?"

"No, ma'am."

"Want to work it too? You can work as many hours as you want."

She sucked in a happy breath and grinned from ear to ear. "Thank you, ma'am!"

"Call me Kylie."

"Yes, ma'am... Kylie."

"Go ahead and get to work." Given that she knew what her job was immeasurably better than I did, I wasn't about to tell her what to do.

I smiled as I watched her disappear into the stock room.

The door's chime pulled my attention back toward the front door.

"Dorothy!" I hissed. If I could have grown venomous fangs, I would have.

"Well!" Dorothy's voice boomed, filling up the very empty café. "Isn't this a sight?" Her smile was mean and her eyes were evil. "I told everybody to stay away from you," she said, sauntering in with an exaggerated hip wag. "Your cooking kills. I told them that. Let them know that you put Dan in the hospital three times."

Dan... Dorothy worshipped the ground he walked on. If she hadn't been his aunt, I was pretty sure that she would have tried to date him.

"Two of those times had been from take-out food," I countered. "And the third time, the doctor said that Dan had an ulcer. It wasn't food poisoning!"

"That's not how I heard it, and that's not how I'm tellin' it."

I wanted to rip her smug smile off her face.

Dorothy crossed her arms over her chest, and her smile fell away to an ugly scowl that creased both sides of her mouth down to her chin. "You had no business coming here, and it's time for you to go. You're going to ruin this place just like you almost drove Dan's business into the ground."

I gaped at her, not believing what I was hearing.

She *tsk*ed and shook her head. "If it hadn't been for that saint of a man always fixing your mistakes behind your back."

Nausea rolled in my stomach and threatened to crawl its way up my neck. "Get out." I pointed at the door behind her. If she didn't leave, I was going to throw her out with my own two hands.

"You never made Dan a decent meal in the eleven years you were married to him. You can't cook, and your food is a danger to the public. I've already told the police. I've warned everyone. Take your failure of a life somewhere else, Kylie. Get out of Camden Falls before you kill someone."

I was so mad I couldn't see straight, let alone think of a comeback. By the time I remembered to breathe, she was already out the door and walking down the sidewalk with a big cheery smile on her face.

I've prided myself in not hating people, but I hated her. I wished I could make her a seven-course meal and make her eat every bit of it just to watch her rush to the hospital afterward to get her stomach pumped.

"I can cook," I seethed. But I couldn't cook. I was terrible at it. Awful. "I will learn how to cook!" My pride surged at the honesty in that declaration.

The café phone rang, and I answered. "Sarah's Eatery."

"You lookin' for a cook?"

Yes! I was still going to learn how to cook, but that didn't mean I knew how to cook today, and it didn't mean I could do everything on my own.

"How soon can you be here for an interview?"

CHAPTER 8

The next week and a half went by in a blur. The first of the month came and went, and my tenants—let me say that again, *my* tenants—lined up to pay me in cash or by check. I wrote them receipts on napkins.

Then it was off to the bank. I opened an account, deposited all of the checks and pocketed the cash. After that, I grabbed an Uber to Walmart and bought a laptop for under $250. I'd seen a few customers using Wi-Fi in the café, so I knew I was good there.

I had yet to pay any of my staff, but that was happening as soon as I saw each and every one of them. That is to say, all three of them.

I closed the café every night, completely

ignoring the times that were listed on the door, and went upstairs, put on my pajamas and then practiced making dinner for myself. I'd set off the fire alarm eight times, made myself sick enough to vomit three times, and had made a not-terrible grilled cheese once.

During the day, Brenda had been cooking enough food to feed any customers who might show up. She'd made spaghetti and meatballs. Spaghetti and meat sauce. Baked spaghetti. And then, finally, breaded and deep fried spaghetti squares. I will never admit to how many times the spaghetti was re-purposed and reused between the various meals, but when Brad, the police officer, came in for a meal for the fifth day in a row, he very politely asked for a to-go cup of soda instead of ordering a meal when he saw the fried spaghetti squares written in my messy scrawl on a menu chalk board.

As for finding a chef, I'd interviewed every single person who had called to ask for an inter-view. I even let an entitled, unexperienced seventeen-year-old high schooler reschedule his interview three times and still listened to what he had to say with an open mind. Yet, some-how, I still thought that he was a better pick than the ego-maniac Italian who told me in no uncertain terms that if he were to accept the job as chef that I would not be allowed inside the kitchen while he was working. Neither would any female wait staff. I took a hard pass on him. It didn't even matter that he could cook. This was my place, my rules, and I was not going to let another man walk into my life and tell me what to do.

After the Italian guy was a local lady who had worked as a cook at the high school for twenty-five years. She might have been a nice person once, but from the way she looked me up and down with her pinched face, sat as far away from me as she could and kept her arms folded across her chest, I had a pretty good idea that we weren't going to work out.

Now I sat in front of another candidate. The café was completely empty except for the two of us, and the bracing, aromatic scent of burnt brownies filled the air. My latest attempt at culinary greatness. I'd even made them from scratch (because I'd run out of brownie mix).

Rachel Summers was about my age. She was slender with high cheekbones, had shoulder-length, light brown hair with strong blonde highlights, a deep, golden tan, and had the tiniest of gaps between her two front teeth. She spoke to me in a way that made me feel as though we'd been friends for the past fifteen years.

She was eager. She was here. She wanted the job.

She couldn't cook. Yet.

I hired her.

"Thank you so much for taking a chance on me," Rachel said as she stood.

I stood as well and accepted her hand to shake. "We can give it a couple of weeks, take things slow, and give your skills a chance to grow." She had to be better than me. Had to be.

"You won't regret this," she said as she followed me to the grill counter.

"I have high hopes." I picked up the brownies intending to throw them in the trash. The smell of burnt chocolate was right up there with the smell of cigarettes.

"Oh!" she said, darting out an arm to stop me. "If... if you don't want those, I'd love to take them."

Brown noser. Check.

I knew that it wasn't necessarily a good quality in a person, but I'd never been considered important enough to be brown nosed to before, and I decided in a flash to enjoy the idolatry while it lasted. Yet my conscience had my hands hanging onto those brownies instead of just handing them over.

"Are you sure you want these? I'd be afraid you'd break a tooth on them." I said it with a laugh, but I really was worried that she could break a tooth. What if she fed them to some unsuspecting kids or someone super elderly? Could I be charged with child abuse or elder abuse just because she got the brownies from me?

Wait. We're in the country. I bet she had a pig. Or chickens. I bet she had chickens. Then I thought about chocolate-flavored eggs and tried not to cringe.

"I'm sure. I have a real weakness for brownies." She reached out her hands with a hopeful look on her face.

Oh my God, she's going to eat them herself. I thought I might cry. With joy. She wanted to eat my cooking! I was going to mark this day on my calendar. Embroider it on a pillow... okay, hire someone to embroider it on a pillow.

"Well, if you're sure..." I let her hands connect with the platter.

"I'll bring the dish back when I start in the morning, if that's okay." Her smile was happy. I had made her happy with burnt brownies. And the polka-dotted platter had "Sarah's Eatery" scrawled in cursive in the center. I knew that there was no way she'd be able to confuse it with one of her own.

"Sure, sure!" I waved her off as she disappeared out the door. I craned my neck and leaned, watching her through the windows for as long as I could, eager to see if she would throw the dish's contents away or toss it into the street for the birds to pick at. Instead, she snuck a little nibble of one of the brownies, taste testing, before cracking off a sizeable wedge. She didn't spit it out or anything.

"Holy cow... she likes my brownies." Suddenly I wasn't sure if hiring her had been a good idea. I mean, if she liked my brownies, what did that say about her flavor palette? The café's food could go from terrible to inhumane.

I looked around at all the empty seats. Taking a risk on her wasn't really that big of a risk. The café couldn't fall much further.

CHAPTER 9

"Y ou've done it! I knew you would," Dorothy, my ex-aunt-in-law declared after slamming through the café's front door. It wasn't even 8 AM yet. A blurry-eyed Zoey sat at the grill's counter nursing a cup of black coffee. Her thick, straight, glossy, black hair was pulled away from her face in a messy half ponytail. Yet, as always, the petite Asian somehow looked flawless, and she didn't even turn her head to acknowledge Dorothy's overly dramatic entrance.

I was pretty sure my ex-aunt-in-law was about to break into song. She was on her stage.

"Good morning, Dorothy. Can I get you a cup of coffee?"

Dorothy's eyes flew wide. She drew her arms up to her chest protectively, hissed, and took a step backward. "And let you poison me too?" Each word was said as if she were spitting.

I glanced at Zoey, then down at her coffee.

Zoey looked at me. "It's pretty good this morning." She shrugged and then took another sip. We both turned our attention to Dorothy, but Brad's entrance in his crisp officer's uniform had me looking past Dorothy at him instead.

Dorothy turned around, saw who had entered, and then literally cackled. I couldn't help it. My eyes darted all around her, expecting a witch's broom to materialize. "You're finally getting yours for all the misery that you put that poor man through. Take her away! Put her in cuffs!"

Brad stopped when he had stepped far enough into the café to be even with her. He wore something akin to a regretful grimace on his face. "Ma'am, I'll need to ask you to leave." Those are the words he said to Dorothy—not to me.

Dorothy sucked in air. Shocked.

I fought the urge to dance.

Brad reached a gentle hand out to her elbow, turned her around and escorted her to the door. He opened the door, guided her through, and then closed the door. There, she stood gape-mouthed, staring in, but Brad turned his back on her and walked with a casual ease to the grill's bar where he sat down on a stool next to Zoey.

"Could I get a cup of coffee, Kylie?"

"Sure!" I had a steaming cup of coffee sitting in front of him a moment later. Next to it I sat a chilled cream dispenser and a bowl filled with sugar cubes.

Brad fixed his coffee with some of both, gave it a stir and then took a sip. "Pretty good this morning."

His compliment had the same effect as putting me on cloud nine. I was sailing.

"You had any luck getting a chef in here yet?"

I glanced at the wall clock behind me before turning back around to face Brad. It was coming right up on 8 AM. "I have. Actually thought she'd be in by now."

"Who'd you hire?" He took another sip.

"Rachel Summers."

He put down his cup of coffee. He didn't say anything for a moment—he just blinked a few times. Then, "I didn't know she could cook."

"She can't, but she said she was willing to work hard at learning." I didn't want to ask how he knew that Rachel couldn't cook. I imagined her butchering an attempt at a cheese omelet to serve up to Brad as a special breakfast for two, and I could feel my little jealousy monster's nails digging into my psyche as she crawled her way out of my depths.

"Rachel's dead, Kylie."

I stretched my neck forward and turned my ear to him a little. I couldn't have possibly heard him right. "Come again?"

"She was found dead last night. A plate of brownies was found next to her."

I was going to be sick right where I stood. I was going to dry heave my empty stomach right in front of my only two customers.

"Bummer," Zoey said before taking another sip of her coffee. Then she turned to Brad. "I feel fine."

Brad gave her a nod. "You are looking better. Any word?"

"Nope. The"—she said what sounded like Mandarin curse words—"has disappeared. He's been using his credit card. I've seen him on some hotel surveillance video. His cell phone is still active and he has accepted phone calls, but none from me."

The title of the books that I'd seen Zoey reading on an earlier day came back to me. *How to Know if He's a Jerk* and *How to Move on After Being Ghosted*. Zoey had been ghosted. She'd had someone in her life who had severed ties with her without even giving her the chance to say goodbye, just as if one or the other of them had died.

Suddenly I saw Zoey with fresh eyes, the way she always looked as though she had been crying or might start crying. She was so young, but she'd experienced something truly awful.

Brad took another sip of his coffee, then asked, "You hacked the hotel cameras and his cell phone records?"

In a completely deadpan fashion, Zoey looked Brad straight in the eyes and answered, "No. Of course not. Not me. Would never." She said it with all the oomph that I might use when reading off the ingredients of a recipe. Eggs. Flour. Butter.

Brad nodded. "That's good to hear." He said as if with complete acceptance of her disavowing having done anything at all wrong, but then his gaze returned to me. "Did you give Rachel brownies, Kylie?"

"Yes." I felt as though my foot were hovering over a bear trap and in the next instance I was going to have to step down into it.

"Did you make those brownies?"

Snap. I all but felt my bones crush.

"Yes." It was the only answer there was to give.

Brad took another sip of his coffee, then stood up. "I need to shut you down pending the results of an investigation. You'll need to lock the café and put up your closed sign. You're not to serve any more customers until further notice."

Zoey took another sip of her coffee. Quiet defiance and unilateral support. I loved her in that moment.

"Am I under investigation for murder?"

There was a slight hesitation before he answered, but when he did answer, there was no hesitation or apology in his voice. "You are a person of interest at this time."

The bear trap snapped again, this time breaking my foot clean off.

CHAPTER 10

*W*hat happened next felt as invasive as anything I'd ever experienced. I might as well have been at the dentist's office with my mouth pried open with fifteen different utensils sticking out of it while the doctor rambled on to a bevy of dental students on the importance of dental hygiene.

I was humiliated.

I was mortified.

I was angry.

Police officers were everywhere, searching through the kitchen and grill. They crouched low, they searched high, and they didn't put anything back where they'd found it. Pots and pans littered the floor. Dishes were stacked on tabletops, and unused tables were turned upside-down as they checked the bottom of the tables and chairs.

"Why are you doing this?" I asked one officer as he trudged past, but instead of answering me, he barked out a question to the collection of officers.

"Why is she in here?" His voice bellowed as if he was yelling through a bullhorn. His shoulders could have withstood an impact from a linebacker, and his hair was in the style of a flat-top bur cut. As gruff as he was, I had to resist the urge to brush my palm over the top of his straight-up hair.

Brad materialized at my side. "I'm keeping an eye on her, Sarge. We don't have a search warrant, but Mrs. Berry gave us permission to search anyway as long as she was allowed to remain present."

"Ms. Berry," I hissed hurriedly under my breath. Regaining the title of "Ms." had been hard, and I wasn't about to let such an oversight pass without saying something.

Sarge, as Brad had called him, humphed and then grumbled something I didn't catch before marching on.

I wondered for the eighteenth time whether

or not I'd made a mistake by allowing them to search the café. A million what-ifs were flooding through my brain. What if I combined the wrong two ingredients and they turned into a poison? Could food even do that? What if I used something in them that I wasn't supposed to? What if I accidentally killed more people? The police were performing a civil service. They were protecting the entire town from me!

"We got something!" a voice from within the walk-in pantry called out. I followed Brad around the long center island as the person who had spoken appeared. He stepped out of the pantry holding an orangeish-yellow box over his head.

It was the baking powder I'd used when baking the brownies. I'd gone old school by not using self-rising flour--not that I'd known what self-rising flour was before I came here. Instead, I'd used all-purpose flour. Self-rising flour already had baking powder added to it, but I'd had to add baking powder myself to the all-purpose flour. The recipe called for that kind of four, so that's what I'd used. I'd done every-thing exactly as the recipe had said, as best as I could understand the instructions.

"Rat poison!" the officer yelled and then slammed the box down on the island counter.

My knees buckled. The only way I stayed standing was Brad's fast arm around me. He pulled me in tight against him, tight enough that I could smell the freshness of his Old Irish soap and the slight smell of starch from his crisp shirt. His body was hard and warm against me, and I wanted to melt into him. I wanted to give him all my troubles and lean against him, but he *was* my troubles. He and his band of merry officers were my personal hunters, and they had me in their sights.

I'd done it. I'd killed that poor, innocent woman. I'd murdered her. The only thing she'd done wrong was answering my ad for a chef. I was about to go away to prison for a very long time.

"Keep searching," Brad instructed the group and everyone regained their focus.

I looked at him, dumbfounded. Why keep looking? They had their murder weapon. Why wasn't I in handcuffs already?

My life would change forever. Once I got to prison, maybe I could "marry" a big butch woman in prison and she could keep me safe. I'd keep the cell nice and tidy. I wouldn't even have to cook for her or worry about children. It could be okay. I could make it work. Did saying you have a headache work with women?

I heard a door open behind me and to the right.

"Where does this door go?" I turned around to the sight of an officer standing at the stairwell doorway.

"That leads to my apartment," I said. How much worse could this day get?

"Do we have your permission to search your apartment?" Brad asked, releasing me to stand on my own. The absence of his body left me feeling cold.

My head was nodding, giving them permission to search before I'd given my head permission to nod.

I led them up the L-shaped flight of stairs and unlocked my door. I then opened the door and stepped aside as a small task force of officers poured in. From there, they scattered. The apartment was almost completely empty, and most of them congregated in the kitchen although some of them headed down the hallway to my bedroom and the bathroom.

I trailed behind, and I felt Brad following. I glanced in the bathroom where two officers were going through the nearly empty vanity. Then, when I reached my bedroom, I found the mattress I slept on turned on its side and the contents of my open suitcase strewn across the floor.

I didn't have to look to know that Brad was standing next to me. He was so incredibly handsome, and now he got to see firsthand the way I was sleeping on a mattress on the floor, just like a homeless person might. The mattress was bare. I didn't even have sheets. I'd been using a long dress as a makeshift blanket to sleep under and a rolled up shirt as my pillow.

My cheeks burned with embarrassment when I felt his gaze on me, but I refused to let my eyes fill with tears. I was in the best living situation I'd been in for months, and by God I would hold my head up high. I would not cry.

CHAPTER 11

*T*he cops were leaving and the café looked as though it had been hit by two tornadoes and a hurricane.

Brad paused beside me, and I took the opportunity to ask what was foremost on my mind. "Why aren't you arresting me?"

"Did you do it?"

"No, I mean, I don't know, but I don't think so." I thought back to that box of rat poison and how I'd thought it was the baking powder when that officer had walked out of the pantry with it. I wish I knew which shelf he'd found it on. That would have given me a much better sense of if I had used it.

"We're aren't arresting you because we don't know what killed Rachel Summers."

"What?" This was news to my ears.

"We know that she died and we suspect that she was eating your brownies when she died and we suspect that the cause of death was poisoning. We don't know what type of poison or how it was ingested."

"So you're saying that you don't have enough evidence to arrest me... yet."

"That's what I'm saying. We're waiting on the coroner's report."

A cold chill washed over me. I had until when they got the coroner's report before they carted me off in handcuffs. I glanced at the clock on the wall above the grill, and I swear that I could hear it ticking from where we stood. My time was running out.

Brad gave me a pat on the shoulder and then followed his fellow officers out the door. When it closed behind him, I was alone.

I turned in a circle looking all around me. The place really was a disaster. They'd left it in shambles, just the way my life was in shambles. I had no idea how I'd managed to go from a terrible situation in Chicago to an even worse situation here. I had to have a voodoo curse on me or something. No one could be this unlucky.

I wanted to go to bed. I wanted to hide my head underneath my blanket-dress and pretend that none of this was happening, but it was only three o'clock in the afternoon and I knew that the café would still look like this when I woke back up. Even so, I couldn't handle staying here. I had to get out.

I decided to go for a walk. But first, I needed to get something to eat. I hadn't eaten anything all day and I was starting to feel light headed. Grabbing a wedge of smoked Gouda cheese from the walk-in cooler, I headed out.

I was wearing black jeans, white sneakers, and a short-sleeve turquoise top that stopped just above the curve of my hips. Outside the sun was warm but the air had a crispness that was emphasized by the soft blowing wind.

There was more traffic than I was used to seeing on Main Street, and I knew that it was because of the time of day. Even at three-thirty, people were starting their transition from their day time life to their evening life. People were picking kids up from school, on their way home from work, or running errands.

As for me, I was simply taking a walk. It felt

like there was nothing in the world left for me to do.

I followed Main Street and passed all of the various businesses. Eventually Main Street curved and the surroundings became more residential. Large, stately houses that looked to be fifty years or more old lined the road with enormous well-kept yards. One house had a wrought-iron fence with pointy spikes on top, and another was made of flat stones that had been lain on top of each other without the use of cement or any other binders.

It was beautiful and peaceful in this neighborhood, and for a moment I imagined that my life had turned out differently. I imagined that I lived here in one of these beautiful houses with a husband who loved me and with children whose days were filled with laughter and play. We had no financial worries, no legal worries, and we were happy.

Out of nowhere a kitten bounced out in front of me, hopping up and down like it was on a pogo stick. Its fur was fluffed up and it was spitting and hissing at me.

I stopped in my tracks, my eyes wide. This apparently hadn't been the response the kitten expected because it quit its hopping, spitting, and hissing and instead rolled onto its back with its talon-like claws stretched and reaching for me.

I still did nothing and this seemed to bore the kitten even more. It sat up prim and proper, looked at me with eyes that seemed both gold and green at the same time and meowed. It had fluffy white and gray fur.

"You want that cat, you can have that cat," a woman's disembodied voice said.

I looked around me. About fifteen feet away, a woman was on her knees planting what I was pretty sure was a rose bush.

"Won't his owner miss him?" I asked.

"Don't have none. It showed up a few weeks back and has been roaming the neighborhood. Teases my dogs through the French doors. I'd be glad to see it gone." She spoke rather matter-of-factly. There was no actual malice in her voice, but it was clear the kitten wasn't wanted.

I broke off a nibble of cheese and gave it a toss toward the kitten. The little guy jumped a foot straight into the air and landed looking like a fur ball, but then inched toward the piece of cheese. It batted it with its paw before going in for a sniff. Finally, it ate it.

"Are you sure no one would miss him?" I asked.

"Positive," the woman called back as she tucked the stumpy rose bush into the ground and started securing soil around it.

Bending over, I dangled my fingers a small ways in front of the kitten. It responded by flopping onto its back and reaching for my fingers with its extended claws. I let the little guy snag me and pull me close enough to gnaw on my fingers while simultaneously raking on my hand with its back claws.

I scooped it up and snuggled it close to my chest. It hissed, sneezed, and then settled into a purr. It didn't even stop purring when I flipped it over for a quick check. The kitten was a little girl.

I smiled over at the lady in her yard, but she was too busy working to notice.

"I'm going to take her home with me, but if anyone wants her back, I'm the new owner of Sarah's Eatery."

The woman looked up from her work, her once pleased face now wearing a heavy scowl. "Oh." Her eyes looked me up and down. "I didn't know."

This time, she didn't return to her work. She

stared at me, her eyes beady and her mouth tight. She made me wonder if I'd grown horns or if maybe I had a booger on the end of my nose.

I looked down at the kitten, and she looked up at me with blissful, half-lidded eyes, and her purr was almost as loud as the traffic driving by. I didn't know why the lady didn't like me, but the kitten did, and that was more than enough.

Not bothering to wave or say goodbye to the woman digging in her yard, I turned around and started the trek back. I had a new friend, and that meant that my life had just gotten a whole lot better. They wouldn't send a new kitten-mommy away to prison. I wouldn't let them. I was sure that I had read every label twice. I wasn't familiar with what was in the pantry, and I was always having to check and recheck what it was that I was about to use. I hadn't even mistaken the salt for sugar. I know that Rachel had died after eating my brownies, but I'd tasted the brownie batter and I felt fine.

I was not the screw up my ex-Aunt Dorothy swore I was.

I was not the throwaway piece of trash my ex-husband had treated me as.

I was a business owner and a new member of this community, and by God, I was going to make them like and accept me even if I had to hire a three-star Michelin chef to do it.

I took another bite of the Gouda cheese and did my best to anchor myself back in reality. A three-star Michelin chef would be way, way, way outside my price range and probably too obnoxious to work with. But I vowed to find another way to win the hearts, trust, and dollars of Camden Falls residents.

I would not give up.

CHAPTER 12

$\mathcal{I}$ headed back to the café with a new friend and a renewed purpose. Save the café. Save myself.

On the way, I passed the office of Attorney at Law Marty Brownwell. His office was somewhat shabby, but clean. He didn't have a secretary, so the person I spoke to was him. He was short and pudgy with a face and body resembling a bulldog, and I imagined him butting heads with the police and managing to stand his ground, so I hired him.

I explained my situation, that the police suspected me of murder and that they had closed down the café pending the results of the investigation. I also explained their lack of evidence and the fact that I had enough money in the bank to pay him... something.

He accepted the job. We shook hands.

When I got back to the café, I dropped my new bestest pal off in my apartment and called an Uber. An hour later I was back with kitty kibble, litter, a litter box, and a how-to book called *Know Your Kitty*. I also picked up an assortment of pre-made cookies, muffins, and even a couple of expertly decorated and scrumptious looking cakes.

I opened a can of tuna and split it between me and my new best pal. "What should I call you?" The kitten looked up at me with her large, luminescent eyes. They looked gold, but then she blinked and they were green. "Sage," I said. "I'll call you Sage."

I extended a hand to pet her but she hunkered down and hissed. I held my hand still, not withdrawing it, and she stood back up and rubbed her cheek against the ends of my fingers.

She was wonderful, everything about her. She was ready to fight, but she was completely open to love.

~

*T*he next morning I opened the café door bright and early for pert Melanie and lanky Sam, both filled with the natural glow that youth gave them. I'd texted them last night and asked them to come help get the café put back in order, and I told them that I would pay them for any scheduled but lost time from yesterday and today, plus extra to cover their loss of tips.

"What a cute little cat!" Melanie exclaimed, making a beeline for the fuzzball in my arms. Sage swatted at her bouncing curls, and then Melanie noticed the space around us and gasped. "What happened?"

"It's not as bad as it looks." That was a bald-faced lie. They hadn't even seen the kitchen yet.

Brenda strolled in ten seconds after Sam and Melanie. "Well!" she exclaimed. "Who'd you make mad?" I knew that she was teasing, but as soon as the words were out, her face fell. "Oh, honey, I'm sorry. I didn't mean nothin'."

"It's okay, Brenda. But I actually have an extra special task for you. Could you make a lasagna?"

"Big enough to feed how many?"

"Uh... a family of four?" I really didn't know the answer.

"Casserole size? Sure," she said, waving a dismissive hand in the air. "I can do that." She headed off toward the kitchen and then a stream of words that had me cupping my hand over sweet, little innocent Sage's ears rang out a moment later.

I cringed. "Melanie, can you go help Brenda put the kitchen back together? I'll help Sam out here."

"Sure," Melanie said with a little laugh in her voice.

The chime on the café door sounded and I turned around to see Zoey walk in.

"I'm sorry, Zoey. I'm not allowed to serve customers yet."

"Then don't charge me." Her steps didn't miss a beat as she headed to the grill's bar and perched on her favorite stool.

I thought about her logic and found it sound. If she wasn't paying, then she was a guest. I went around to the grill-side of the counter and started a pot of coffee.

"You know, if you served coffee from individual French presses you could charge more for it."

I paused mid coffee scoop. Zoey had a point. I could sell servings of coffee by the quarter, half or full French press. People were passionate about good coffee, and I knew there had to be some reason why French presses were considered special. Grabbing a pen, I made a note of it on a napkin. "Thanks, Zoey!"

By 10 AM, Agatha waltzed in as the aged empress that she was accompanied by a loyal entourage of two other women. Each one of them had a large tote of one kind or other on their arm, and none of them seemed to take notice of the big closed sign I had hung on the door. Instead, Agatha waved and called good morning as the group made their way to the sunny back nook with its cozy, oversized chairs. There, they got out their knitting and chattered as they worked. Nearby, Sage slept, curled up and content.

Without being asked, I served them three cups of coffee with a side of chilled cream and sugar cubes along with a plate of store-bought sugar cookies and pecan sandies. "No customers today, ladies, so this is on the house. Enjoy."

They cooed over the offering as their fingers flew, never missing a stitch.

Just before noon, more would-be customers came in for lunch. I presented them with glasses of milk or coffee and a slice of store-bought double chocolate fudge cake. Again on the house, and again, nobody complained.

The door of the café burst open and my heart stuttered in my chest, afraid that the police had come to bust me for serving food to people. But the newcomer was none other than Marty Brownwell. To my great relief, he was wearing a triumphant smile and he was holding a piece of paper in the air tight in his pudgy hand.

I hurried over to him while trying not to be as obvious as breaking into a mad dash. "Did you do it?"

"I sure did!" He slapped the paper against the palm of his other hand before handing it over to me. "The injunction against the café has been lifted as an undue hardship without proof of wrongdoing." He glanced around us at the various "customers" who had gathered. "You can now legally sell your goods."

I'd never been a hugger, but I did just that. I threw my arms around Mr. Brownwell's neck and jumped up and down. Mr. Brownwell wasn't much taller than me, and my antics jostled him all about while tears of joy stung my eyes. Until that moment, I'd had no idea how much the café meant to me.

He blushed when I gave him a kiss on the cheek and gave me an *aww, shucks* schoolboy look.

Turning around to face the café, I held the piece of paper over my head and yelled out at the top of my lungs, "We're open for business!" The small chorus of whoops and clapping that reached me might as well have been made by a stadium full of ecstatic fans as far as I was concerned.

I flipped the closed sign to open.

Save the café... Check. I mentally crossed it off my list.

Save myself... That was coming next.

CHAPTER 13

I leaned over the lasagna that Brenda had made and breathed it in deep. It looked and smelled delicious. It bubbled with gooey cheese, and I could just make out the tangy scent of the tomato sauce. My mouth was watering, and I had to fight myself to keep from cutting out a serving… to taste test.

Nearby, Melanie was rinsing some dishes and loading them into the industrial strength dishwasher. We'd had so few customers that we only had to run the dishwasher once a day ever since I'd taken over.

"Melanie, I'd like to take this lasagna to Rachel's family, but I don't know where she lived or anything about her family. Do you know anything?"

Melanie paused in her work, thinking. "No, but I'm sure that the newspaper guy would know. Joel."

I thought back to my first day when Sarah had introduced me to all of her regulars. Joel had been the kind seeming, lumberjack of a guy. I hadn't seen him since that day, and my heart fell a little that one of Sarah's regulars had given up on the café already. "Do you know where I can find him?"

"The newspaper office is on Waters Street, two streets behind Main Street and a couple of blocks over."

In walking distance. "Thanks, Melanie!" I knew that it wasn't much of an offering, but I put together an assortment of cookies on a plate and then covered it with plastic wrap. I wished I had a basket to carry it in but opted for a left-over grocery bag instead.

Leaving the café in Melanie and Sam's capable hands, I set out on foot. It was a beautiful day. The more time I spent in the sleepy little town of Camden Falls, the more I grew to appreciate it. People looked less rushed than they had in Chicago, and while I couldn't say for sure, I thought they looked happier, too. They certainly looked less stressed. People smiled more here. Okay, maybe they didn't smile at me once they knew who I was, but I did see more smiles in general.

Stopping, I looked at the metal inlaid sign above the door of a stone building. The sign read "Camden Falls Herald."

Pushing in the glass front door, an electronic chime announced my arrival rather than a tinkling physical bell like the one attached to the café's front door. A half-square counter encased me into the entryway and stopped me from going any further. Beyond that was a wall with a single doorway. Its door was partially open, but I couldn't see anything past it. There was no one in sight.

"Hello?" I called out. I heard movement and then Joel appeared in the doorway. The whole doorway. His head was half a foot from touching the top and his shoulders nearly touched both sides of the door frame. I'd thought he was a big man when I'd seen him sitting down in the café, but now he put me in mind of Paul Bunyan. He was a giant.

Then he smiled. His eyes crinkled, and my heart melted. I had to catch myself in a sigh.

Something about him made me want to curl up on the couch in a snuggly blanket and tell him my whole life story.

Shaking my head, I did my best to break out of his spell, but then my eyes focused on him and I was smiling and inwardly sighing all over again.

"Hi," he said. His warm voice washed over me, and I got goosebumps.

He stepped up to the counter and I had to crane my head back in order to look up at him. "How tall are you?" I asked with awe in my voice. My cheeks heated at asking such a personal question, but the words just popped out of my mouth.

He chuckled and butterflies did looping swirls in my stomach. "Six-five."

I blinked. That made him a foot and a quarter taller than me, and I had no doubts that he would be able to wrestle a bull to the ground if we were to go on a picnic and, you know, get surprised by a rampaging bull...

I had to shake my head again and force myself to snap out of it. I was newly divorced, newly burned—new to shunning all men because they were men!

I inwardly sighed again, sure that I was

getting all dreamy-eyed once more despite my best efforts to the contrary.

"Is there anything that I can help you with?"

It was a simple enough question but I died a little when he asked it. I was mortified at my schoolgirl behavior while he was all business.

"Do I smell cookies?"

Again, a simple enough question, but it made me want to jump for joy. I no longer felt like a complete idiot. "Yes!" How he could smell them past the grocery bag and beneath the plastic wrap I had no idea. Now I wondered at having used my shampoo as a body wash that morning. It was apple-scented. If he could smell me, hopefully he thought I'd been baking amazing apple pies all morning.

I lifted the bag to the counter and unveiled the plate of sugar, pecan sandies, and chocolate chip cookies. Unwrapping the plate, I slid it across the counter to him. I couldn't stop my grin when he bit into one of the sandies and closed his eyes in pleasure.

"I'm sorry I haven't been by the café since Sarah left," he said after swallowing.

The elephant stepped into the room and sounded its call. I hadn't planned on bringing it up, but I was glad that he did. "I know that it's been a big change." My heart skipped a beat as a thought flashed into my head. He was quite a bit younger than Sarah, but maybe they had once been sweethearts and he'd been sad to see her go. Sounding half-hearted even to my own ears, I said, "I know that the café won't be the same without her."

$\mathcal{H}$e smiled bright. "It takes time! I took this place over from my uncle. You'll eventually make it your own."

Make it my own...

"You could even change the name."

Change the name...

It was such a revolutionary thought. Changing the name had never occurred to me. "I don't have to sell the same foods that Sarah did." I said it like an epiphany, and I thought about Zoey's suggestion of selling coffee by the French press. "I could change the menu." I didn't know why it was such an amazing concept for me to wrap my mind around. It wasn't like I'd been following Sarah's menu since I'd arrived. I didn't have a chef and I didn't have the personal skills to make any of the dishes she'd made the café famous for. I'd been serving spaghetti in all the various forms that Brenda had made it.

Another thought hit me. I was going to be out of business soon if I didn't turn things around! People were going to get tired of eating spaghetti day in and day out. It wasn't about my ex-Aunt Dorothy or the police. It was all me. I was failing at running the café. No one else was ruining it for me. It was all me!

I looked up into Joel's dark honey eyes. "Thank you!" His grin was my answer of *you're welcome*.

"Is there anything I can do for you? Did you want to take out an ad?"

Advertising! I felt like palming myself in the forehead. I had handled nearly every aspect of my ex-husband's business, yet I was managing the café like some sort of business novice. First chance I got, I needed to draw up a business plan.

I glanced down at the plate of cookies and rewound all my thoughts in order to recall why I'd sought Joel out. It was then that I remembered. "The police think that I murdered Rachel Summers," I blurted.

Joel chuckled again, and I hoped that it was because my candor amused him and not because I was making an enormous fool of myself.

"Did you kill her?"

I sucked in a breath of air as I considered his choice of words. I had said murdered. I definitely had not murdered her, but if I used the rat poison instead of baking powder, I most definitely could have killed her.

"I don't know," I finally answered honestly.

He nodded sagely, but when he didn't speak, a silence followed that sucked more words out of me.

"I would like to take a lasagna to her family." One of his eyebrows quirked and I quickly added, "I didn't make it. Brenda made it." More silence, then more words from me. "Problem is, I don't know anything about Rachel or even where she lived. Could you help me with that?"

Nodding some more and with a twinkle of humor in his eyes, he said, "I can help you with that."

CHAPTER 14

*M*elanie had been right. Joel had been the man-in-the-know, and now I was standing outside of Rachel's townhouse with a heavy lasagna cradled in my arms as my Uber driver drove away. But, it wasn't just Rachel's townhouse. It was actually a townhouse duplex, and according to Joel, the other side was owned by Rachel's sister, Veronica.

I walked up the concrete walkway to the double front doors, contemplating on which one to knock. The left door had a decorative fall wreath filled with pine cones and colorful leaves. The other door was blank. The door with the wreath also had a welcome mat, but the mat in front of the other door didn't have any welcoming words on it.

I stepped to the left and gave the decorated door a hearty rap with my knuckles. The sound of screaming children grew until there was a loud thump from the other side of the door, followed by more screaming. Then, there was a woman's voice.

"Scoot! Get away from there. It could be the boogieman! You know you're not allowed to open the door. Go on, go out back."

More screaming, this time drifting away from the door.

The door opened and I plastered a huge, strained smile on my face. It was so big and so false that it hurt my cheeks.

"Yes?" The woman asked as she looked me over from head to toe and back up again. She was wearing shorts and a loose knit shirt without any shoes. Her hair looked as though it had been bleached blonde three times too many. That is to say, it looked like white straw.

"Hi, my name is Kylie Berry, and..." I hadn't thought this through. What was I supposed to say—hello, I'm the woman who killed your sister? I choked a little and then cleared my throat, ready to try again. "I'm the new owner of Sarah's Eatery."

Veronica's eyes narrowed and her lips pursed. She shifted her weight so that her hip stuck out, and she propped her hand on it with her elbow jutting out. "What you got there?" she asked, her eyes flicking to the tinfoil covered casserole dish in my arms.

"It's a lasagna." My voice squeaked, but I stood my ground. "My assistant, Brenda, made it. I didn't make it."

Veronica's pursed lips lifted into a smile. "Well come on in here." She waved me in, and I followed her to the kitchen. I put the lasagna on the counter, and she whipped the top off. Leaning over to breathe it in, she hummed her satisfaction with half-lidded eyes.

"Nice," she said.

She got out two plates and cut two pieces, one for me and one for her. She handed out the forks, and it was not lost on me that she waited for me to take a bite before she did.

Next to me were sliding glass doors that opened to a lovely backyard. There, the kids were playing. There was a divider fence between her yard and what I assumed was her sister's yard. I was a little surprised to discover that they didn't share one large backyard.

"Mmmmm, this is good," Veronica said. "You know the best thing about it?"

I shook my head no.

"I didn't have to make it!" She slapped the counter as she laughed at her own joke. It made me feel pretty good. It made me feel like maybe she wasn't going to chase me from her home with a meat cleaver.

"Veronica, I just wanted to say how sorry I am about your loss." I studied her face. Her eyes weren't bloodshot from crying or lack of sleep. Her house looked as though she'd been cleaning recently. And the kids looked pretty happy. Of course, they were kids and kids were resilient, so...

Still, her sister and their aunt had just died. I wasn't noticing any grieving going on.

"You know what," Veronica said conspiratorially in answer to my offer of condolence, "things happen." She took a bite of lasagna, and I got the impression that she didn't have any more to say on the matter. She seemed at peace.

"But the brownies came from me." I knew I was poking a bear, but I needed to know what was going on. There was something about the situation that I wasn't understanding.

"Oh, those brownies!" Veronica exclaimed, her eyes wide. "They looked so good! When I went next door to ask Rachel what she had done with my favorite hoodie jacket and saw those brownies sitting there"—she gasped, throwing her hands in the air as she rolled her eyes back in her head, kind of like she'd died and gone to heaven—"I almost snuck one for myself. Rachel was laying back in her lawn chair sleeping—well, I thought she was sleeping—and I was soooo tempted." She sobered. "But I didn't."

She'd said that the brownies had looked good. She'd wanted one. Badly. I knew that taste was a subjective experience and there was someone somewhere who liked anything a person could imagine. Maybe both the sisters enjoyed burnt brownies.

I glanced down at the lasagna we were sharing. It was really delicious, but it was not burnt. Maybe their taste for burnt foods only applied to pastries... or maybe just chocolate.

"I'm so glad to hear that you liked how they looked. I haven't been cooking for very long, I mean, not professionally."

Veronica laughed. "To listen to that aunt of yours talk, you can't cook at all!"

I felt my face heat.

"Oh, I'm just teasing you, darlin'." She gave me a conciliatory pat on the arm. "Them brownies looked real fine. You did a real good job." Her face scrunched. "You know what I mean."

"Veronica." My voice went up two octaves when I said her name, and I made a point of dropping it back down. "Were things okay between you and your sister?"

"Why?" Veronica put her fork down with a clatter and leaned forward aggressively. "What have you heard?"

"N-nothing. You all seem so, um, well-adjusted. I have to admit that I'm a little confused."

Veronica's face twisted up some more, but then it relaxed. "Truth be told, my sister was a pill—bitter, hard to swallow, and bad for your health. Any time she wanted her way, she'd threaten to tell my children that Santa Claus i'nt real. Now who does that? Who threatens to hurt little babies just 'cause they want to be a baby who always gets their way?" She took another bite of the lasagna. She chewed angrily and then swallowed angrily. "That woman used up every one of my last nerves. She was my sister and I was supposed to love her. I know that. And God is gonna judge me when I get up to heaven and He knows I didn't love her, but she done used up all the love I had for her years ago."

Oooh... I was starting to get a tad bit of clarity. If Rachel had used up her sister so thoroughly, there was no telling what she'd done to other people.

I decided to make a leap of logic. "Veronica, about those brownies, were they burnt?"

Veronica scrunched her face and snorted with derision. "Them brownies weren't burnt. They were perfect."

Bingo... The brownies that Rachel was eating at the time she died weren't *my* brownies. I didn't kill her!

As my thoughts tumbled over each other, a slight pause in the conversation happened. I took a breath to speak, but Veronica jumped back in.

"And it weren't just me that felt that way about her, I want you to know. She was so manipulative, so greedy. She didn't think twice about doing somebody wrong."

I was so thrown. The woman she was describing didn't sound anything like the woman I had interviewed to be the new chef at Sarah's Eatery. But I guessed that's what manipulative people were like. They could fool you into thinking the way they wanted you to think so that they could get you to do whatever it was that they wanted you to do.

"Back six months ago," Veronica continued, "Rachel had some woman over at her place screaming at her at four in the morning. I thought about calling the cops, but the more I heard of what that poor woman had to say, the more I thought that it was best to let Rachel get what was coming to her. Something about 'stay away from my fiancé' and Rachel yelling, 'You're too fat to keep a man like that.' Back and forth, back and forth, until I finally had to put some music on in the kids' rooms to drown out all the yelling."

"Do you know who it was that was yelling at Rachel?"

"I looked out the upstairs window but all I could see was a woman with strawberry blonde hair and dark roots. And she was a little heavy but she was still cute. Rachel had no business talking to her that way. Finally, Rachel yelled that the woman was so ugly that she'd never find any other man and because of that Rachel would take pity on her and stay away from her fiancé."

Tingles ran all up and down my spine.

I had a new lead for my investigation!

CHAPTER 15

*W*hen I got back to the café, Melanie had already left and Sam was just waiting for me to get back. Brenda had taken off hours ago.

Sam had his things together and was ready to go when I walked in.

"Thanks, Sam," I said holding the door open for him. I was pretty sure he had an evening study group he had to get to.

"See you tomorrow, boss!" he said as he rushed out the door with a backpack slung over his shoulder.

I had to smile at that. I really did like the sound of that.

I took care of the rest of the customers the

best I could for the rest of the night. Meaning, I made them peanut butter and jelly sandwiches and served them store-bought cookies and cake. I sold everything at cost, and I prepared everything at the grill where everyone in the café could see me. My name wasn't cleared of wrongdoing yet. I was still a suspect in a murder investigation, even if I now knew that I couldn't have been the one to kill Rachel. Just because I knew it didn't mean that anybody else knew it, and I didn't want to give anyone the chance to say that I'd made a similar mistake again.

The café emptied out about eight-thirty. I locked the door and headed upstairs with little Sage. She stretched herself upward and rested her chin on my shoulder as I unlocked the apartment door to let us both in. As soon as we'd made it inside, she sprang to life and leaped down from her perch. I heard her crunching at her food dish a moment later.

I went to bed tired but I fell asleep with a smile on my face. Little by little, I was getting my life back, and tomorrow, I was going to find out who that woman with the strawberry-blonde hair was.

"Jack," I said, warming up his coffee with a splash of newly brewed coffee. "Did you know Rachel Summers by any chance?"

Jack lifted his bald head to look at me over the top of his newspaper. His dark eyes were two shades darker than his skin. "Can't say I did." He disappeared behind the paper again, but then reappeared a moment later. "Her sister's husband did come to me for a loan a few weeks back, though."

I picked up a towel and started mindlessly wiping down the counter in front of him. "Oh, yeah? I didn't realize you work at the bank."

"Well, one *does* often work at the establishment that one owns." Jack folded the paper in his lap and took a sip of his coffee.

Owned the bank? That certainly explained his stylish and immaculate suits.

I studied the spot that I was rubbing with the towel. It was clean enough, but I kept rubbing it. What I was about to ask was so inappropriate that it made me uncomfortable, but I asked anyway. "Did you give him the loan?"

Jack laced his long fingers, put his elbows on the counter and leaned his chin on his hands before giving a small shake of his head. "No."

I was surprised he told me, but I wasn't going to pass up the opportunity to learn all that I could. Learning what I could from him could mean the difference between restoring some value to my name and going to prison.

I stopped rubbing the counter top and met Jack's gaze. "Would you be able to tell me why he needed the loan?"

Jack shook his head again. "No." Pause. "But I can tell you that getting the loan was a matter of high need."

"But you didn't give him the loan..."

"That's correct."

If Jack didn't give Victoria's husband a loan, that must mean that the bank didn't deem him to be a sound financial risk. They were concerned he wouldn't be able to pay the loan back. And if they were concerned that he might not be able to pay the loan back, that could mean that he was already financially over-extended. On top of that, Jack had said that the loan was of "high need." Getting that loan had been important to Victoria and her husband.

I got more tingles up my spine as another

piece of the puzzle slipped into place. Victoria and her husband were having money problems. If Victoria was set to inherit from Rachel, then Rachel's death could have benefited them financially at a time when they really needed it. But would the greedy and malicious Rachel have been willing to leave her sister anything? Her death might not have helped Victoria at all.

"Thanks, Jack!" He'd given me a lot to think about.

I stepped away out of Jack's line of sight and made a note on a napkin. *Veronica --> financial gain.* There, I'd listed the suspect and the motive.

I shoved the napkin into my pocket but then pulled it out again almost as fast. I wrote, *Get small notebook,* and then folded and shoved the napkin back in my pocket again.

Agatha and her knitting friends were in the cozy alcove again. It was set up as a comfy, quiet spot with oversized cushioned chairs and even had a small wood stove fireplace tucked diagonally in the corner. The spot was designed like a reading nook.

I took the ladies a plate of cookies and a family-style bowl of spaghetti and meatballs, made by Brenda that morning. I also took them a small stack of bowls and the necessary utensils.

"On the house, ladies," I said, perching on the edge of a large chair, forcing Sage to share it with me. I had to quit giving food away, but this time was okay. It was for a good cause. I was hunting a killer.

"Oh thank you, dear," Agatha said. She was working on an afghan made up of soft creams and grays. "This is Nancy and Shelly. They're sisters." Agatha had given a nod to the woman closest to me when she'd said Nancy and to the other one when she'd said Shelly.

"Hi," I said with a wave of my hand. The sisters looked to be in their late 60s or early 70s, and even though they were both sitting down, I could tell that they were exceptionally tall with long legs, and I could see their family resemblance in their long faces and long noses. They both had light brown hair that was cut short, but it was nowhere close to being as short as Agatha's brilliantly white pixie cut. Nancy was knitting light blue socks, and Shelly was knitting a charcoal gray toboggan.

I had never in my life been a gossip, and working up the nerve to ask these ladies to tell me about people not present went against every fiber of my being, but I did it anyway. "I was hoping to learn more about Rachel. Do you know if she was friends with—or knew—a strawberry-blonde or someone a little overweight?"

I addressed the question collectively to the group. I didn't want to leave anybody out.

"I heard that Rachel couldn't keep a man," Nancy said with a critical brow lifted. "She'd keep 'em for a while, be sweeter than sweet to them, but then things would always sour and the feller would go off to wherever he came from."

That certainly seemed to support what I'd learned from Veronica about Rachel's proclivity toward borrowing men from wherever or whomever she pleased, or at least it didn't contradict it.

Shelly spoke up next. "I don't know anything about a strawberry-blonde, though. Are you asking about a woman?"

"Yes," I said.

It was Nancy's turn again. "I don't think Rachel had any female friends." Her sister nodded in silent agreement.

I turned my attention to Agatha. "Do you know anything about her?"

"No, I don't, sweetie, other than to say that if you did kill her you apparently did the world a favor. People always speak well of the dead, but I haven't heard one person say a genuinely kind word about her. But enough about that. We are having our book club tonight, and I want you to come."

I opened my mouth and closed it a couple of times before figuring out what to say. It was such a hard left turn. On one hand, I could be wasting valuable investigative time if I attended the book club meeting. But on the other hand, attending that type of community event could help me win new customers for the café and give me the opportunity to learn more about Rachel and who might have wanted to do her permanent harm.

I smiled, suddenly eager even though I'd felt unsure a heartbeat before. "I'd love to come." Then my smile dropped away and gravity took over the corners of my lips. "But what if I haven't read the book? What is the book?"

Agatha's eyes twinkled mischievously. "*To Kill a Mockingbird.*"

Ohhhh, Agatha was one I'd have to watch. She was having way too much fun with this,

and I wondered if they'd picked their book
before or after Rachel died.

"Where are you having it?"

"Right here."

Ohhhh—again!

I wasn't able to hold my laughter back. "I
guess it's settled! I'll come!"

CHAPTER 16

I knew it was silly, but I didn't want to go to the book club alone. I asked Jack just as he was leaving where I might find Zoey, and he pointed me across the street and a few buildings down. Apparently she had an apartment above a business, the same as I did.

Leaving the café in Melanie's hands, I went across the street and looked for a way to reach Zoey's apartment upstairs. I was really hoping that I wouldn't have to go snooping through the insides of the various businesses below. Finally, I spotted a door with a small window that showcased a set of stairs just beyond.

I tried the door. Unlocked.

The stairs were narrow, dark, and uninviting, but I followed them up anyway. Once I reached the top, instead of finding a single apartment door, like I had at the top of my stairs, I instead found a hallway with seven doors, four on one side and three on the other. These apartments were sure to be much smaller than mine.

I was pretty sure that Zoey worked from home, so I walked the hallway, listening for sounds of life beyond each door. I only heard sound coming from one door, and it was that of an anguished soprano singing in what I could only guess was Italian. I tapped on the door, timidly at first, but then knocked harder a second time when I didn't get an answer.

The music stopped, and the door opened. I'd found Zoey.

I wasn't sure how she managed to look defiant by just standing there, but she did. It wasn't in her stance, and she hadn't said a word, yet she looked as though she could easily destroy the world and not give it a second thought afterward. Her almond-shaped eyes were given startling emphasis with heavy black cat-eye eyeliner that highlighted her natural exotic beauty. Her lips were glossed with blood-red lipstick. She looked like a superhero minus the full-body leotard, and she was every bit as imposing. Instead, she wore cutoff jean short-shorts with black tights topped with what looked like a man's baby-blue, button-up shirt that was tied at the waist.

I suddenly had doubts about my choice for a book club partner, but not because of how she was dressed. She looked fabulous and fierce. No, I was having doubts because of her unimpressed expression at seeing me on her doorstep.

Zoey looked me over from head to toe. "Where are my cookies?"

"What?"

"I saw you carrying a bag of stuff down the street yesterday. You went to the Herald. When you came out you didn't have the bag anymore." Her eyes narrowed. "I think you took Joel cookies. Where are my cookies?"

How did she know about the cookies?

I stared at her a second and then I leaned a little to the side to look into Zoey's dark apartment. Over her shoulder I could see a half-circle of eight or nine monitors stacked two layers tall. They were all on, and a couple of them skipped between various views of what I believed were the streets of Camden Falls.

"You have cameras hidden around town?" I asked, feeling incredulous despite what I was seeing.

"No! Of course not." She hooked a thumb over her shoulder to point at the monitors. "This is video feed that I capture from the stoplights and the various business maintained surveillance cameras around town."

"Oh." I was a little stunned, but then a flash of excitement shot through me. "Do you have anything that could clear me of Rachel's murder?"

"Nooo, I'm sorry. I looked." She sounded genuinely regretful, and I realized I had a friend. I had come to the right place after all.

"I want you to come with me to Agatha's book club meeting tonight," I announced.

Zoey shrugged. "Okay."

That went much easier than I ever imagined.

A *ding* sounded from within the depths of the room, grabbing Zoey's instant attention. She whirled around and hurried to the monitors.

I knew that I hadn't been invited in, but I took the absence of telling me to stay out plus the door she'd left open as an unspoken allowance of my presence within her home. I followed her in.

She was standing in front of her crescent moon of monitors, bent at the waist, staring intensely at the image on the bottom, left-most screen. The monitor showed a man walking down the street, and a mesh of computerized lines covered his face in a variety of geometric shapes.

Zoey did something, and the image zoomed in on the man's face, providing a close-up. She froze the image. "It's not him." There was utter defeat in her voice, and she sat down heavily in her desk chair. Her shoulders sagged.

I looked around me, found an empty milk crate that was doubling as a vinyl records holder, and slid it closer to use as a low stool. I sat down, looked at Zoey, and waited.

Slouched in her chair, Zoey blew out a breath. The sadness in her face aged her by ten years, making her look over thirty instead of her usual barely-twenty. "Max Hamilton. He was—is... I don't know—my fiancé. I moved to this town for him. He'd been here several times and had fallen in love with it, so when we got engaged, he wanted us to use this as home base. He's a sports talent scout."

"You haven't seen him in a while?" My heart

was dropping into my stomach for what she'd been through.

"Nope, at least not through his voluntary doing. I'm using a face recognition program to monitor Camden Falls, and I monitor as many towns as I can where there have been reports of promising talent." She shook her head and rolled her eyes. "I know he's alive, that no one is holding him hostage. I've got glimpses of him a few times, and I've been able to monitor some of his credit card activity. I have reason to believe that he's even using the same cell phone with the same cell phone number, but when I call him the phone either rings... or it goes to voicemail after just a ring or two."

There was a lot of hurt in her voice when she said this last part, and I understood why. If the phone was ringing but cut off suddenly to go to voicemail, it meant that Max had the phone in hand and was pressing the ignore button instead of the answer button.

"I'm so sorry, Zoey."

She shook her head. "I can't believe I fell for someone like him. I can't believe I didn't see this coming. I sold everything that wouldn't fit in my car and drove down here on my own because he was on the road. I was supposed to get an apartment set up for us, and I even signed a rental agreement on a place that I couldn't afford on my own. Then I started planning our wedding. He would sweep into town and we'd have an amazing weekend or sometimes even a week together, but any time I had questions about the wedding planning, he'd always say, 'Whatever you want.' Then it came time for me to start locking down dates with deposits, and he told me to go ahead and pay and he'd wire me some money. Then, when I'd ask him about it, he'd say he forgot to send it but he'd do it right away. He didn't even help pay the deposit on the apartment. I got stressed out, then he got stressed out. He'd end our calls early. Then," she shrugged, "he stopped answering my calls and he stopped calling at his usual times."

She stared off into the shadows of her apartment before going on. "It's not really about the money. I know I'm making it sound like it is. I trusted him. I went out on a limb because he told me to. He told me to trust him, and I did. I really, really did. I never second-guessed his intentions. I always thought that he wanted the best for me and would be there for me. But it's been six months since I've heard his voice, and trusting him meant that I had to max out three different credit cards. I never thought that he'd do this to me. Not for a second."

She sniffed and wiped a tear from the corner of her eye before continuing. "And the worst of it is that I've got no closure. We never broke up. The last time we talked he told me he loved me, that he couldn't wait to marry me, and that he'd be home that weekend. He made me laugh and feel like everything was okay, and then... It's like I stopped existing for him."

I'd never given my husband food poisoning despite what my ex-Aunt Dorothy said, but I would sure try to give it to Max Hamilton if I ever met him. I couldn't imagine the pain that he had caused Zoey, and it was clear that it had lingered like a phantom limb. If he'd simply broken up with her, she would have been able to process her grief. Instead, she was left trying to make sense of two completely different sets of information. There were the memories of her fiancé making her feel special, valuable and important, and then there was all of the inferred information brought on by his absence that implied just the opposite. But that second set of information existed without any confirmation to make it strong enough to stand up against the original memories that he'd forged with her.

"So he's why you were reading those books soon after I first met you?" I asked.

"*How to Know if He's a Jerk* and *How to Move on After Being Ghosted*? Yeah, he's why. I've been trying to sort it all out, and I've been trying to find him." She motioned to the monitors. "I just need some closure."

I blew out a heavy sigh, wishing there was something I could do for her.

"So what's your story?" Zoey asked, turning her gaze on me.

"Huh?"

"I caught it on surveillance. You got to town in a fancy car that was running out of gas, and then abandoned the car and left the keys in the trunk. Then, you walked over a mile to get to the café, all while wearing high heels and dragging a suitcase behind you."

I nodded. That had been a hard day... and an amazing day. "My husband and I got a divorce. We'd been married for eleven years, since I was eighteen." I shook my head. "I'd been young and in love, so when he gave me the prenup to sign, I just signed it. So, eleven years later when I found out that he'd had as many girlfriends while we'd been married as I had toes and fingers, he got everything and I got nothing." It was my turn to shrug.

"Men really are jerks," she said.

I shrugged again. "I gotta believe that there's some good ones out there. I still have hope."

"Then you're a better person than me."

"I don't think so. I've just had more of a chance to heal, but I know you'll get there."

Zoey nodded as she turned her attention back toward the monitors, searching them for a ghost. "Yep, just as soon as I make someone else need some mighty healing as well."

CHAPTER 17

*A*s promised, Zoey came over that evening for book club. The café was empty except for a group of ladies ranging in age between what I guessed was late thirties to Agatha, Agatha being a timeless creature who seemed to defy all logic. She walked with the easy gait of a teenager, had the deft hands of a wizened doctor, and the sharp eye and wit of a stand-up comedienne.

Zoey and I were by far the youngest in attendance.

When Zoey showed, she appeared to be of a lighter spirit than all the times I'd seen her before, and I thought that maybe our conversation had done her heart some good. Her smile finally reached her eyes.

"Can I offer anyone anything else?" I asked as I set down a platter of peanut butter and jelly sandwiches that I'd cut into finger food-sized squares alongside a plate of cookies. Everyone already had coffee or milk. I hadn't worked my nerve up to serve sweet tea yet. I had no idea how to make it, and I was terrified that if I served instant tea that I might get laughed out of town. Even the local fast food restaurants boasted having freshly brewed sweet tea.

"This looks lovely," Agatha praised. I knew she was being generous.

The ladies had already re-arranged the reading nook to include some of the regular table chairs amid the cozy armchairs, and additional chairs were used between some of the members as side tables. Seeing the makeshift nature of the arrangement made me embarrassed that I didn't have a proper coffee table to offer as a centerpiece on which to put drinks and individual plates of food, and I mentally added it to the list of things I wanted to change about the café.

"Allow me to make introductions," Agatha said. She crossed her legs and then lay her long, elegant hands over her knees. "Kylie and Zoey, this is everyone. Everyone, this is Kylie and Zoey. Kylie is under investigation for the murder of Rachel Summers."

I choked on air, but everyone else in the group merely snickered. I glanced hurriedly around me in search of malicious delight, but all I saw was good-humored fun. I relaxed, and the hard tension that drained away from my shoulders actually left my muscles sore.

"Now, who read the book *To Kill a Mockingbird*?" Agatha demanded to know.

There was a chorus of answers, all in the affirmative that the book had been read.

Zoey and I glanced at each other. I had no idea what the book was about. I had hoped that I would not be alone in my ignorance, but Zoey quickly chimed in, "I was impressed with little Scout's maturity."

Instantly, there were more murmurs of assent.

I wanted to crawl off into a hole for being the only one who knew nothing about a book that had long been heralded for its literary genius. That I'd only been invited to the book club meeting earlier that day didn't seem to matter to my pride.

Despite that, to my great fortune the word "kill" was right there in the book's title, and Agatha had announced my connection with Rachel Summers' death. That is to say, the possibility that I'd murdered her. So, there was no need for me to tiptoe around the subject.

I could sleuth to my heart's content.

"I'm Paula," one of the ladies announced. She had a baby fat quality to her puffy cheeks that made her look heavy when in fact she was actually very slender with long, delicate wrists and ankles. "I thought that the lawyer, Atticus, was noble but depressing at the same time."

The group flew into a discussion about that.

"I'm Rita," another woman said, introducing herself. She wore Harry Potter-like glasses and had very large teeth. When she spoke, she put me in mind of a college-educated beaver. "I was so glad to see that Bob Ewell git stuck by that Boo Radley!"

There was a chorus of very hearty agreement.

"And when they killed that mockingbird!" I exclaimed, determined not to be left out.

You could have heard a pin drop. Everyone went silent. Then I heard it—a snicker. Then another and another until the women were laughing so hard that their faces had gone red and some were holding their sides or grasping at the person next to them to keep from falling out of their chair.

Zoey leaned over to me. "They didn't kill any mockingbirds in the story, at least not literal ones."

I felt my face heat with embarrassment, but this time I refused to let myself be undone by it. I forged in after the laughter died down to a few titters. "I didn't read it. That's pretty obvious. Agatha was kind enough to invite me to the group earlier this afternoon, and I wanted to come."

"We're glad to have you," a woman with curly auburn hair said as she wiped a laughter tear from her eye. Nobody at the meeting had strawberry-blonde hair. "We don't care what your aunt says about you."

"That woman has sucked one too many lemons," Agatha added.

"You all know Dorothy?" I asked. I hated how much that woman had been messing with my life. I'd never done anything to her. All the years that I'd been married to Dan, I'd been nothing but nice to her while she had fawned over every word that came out of his mouth. I swear, had he farted she would have called it perfume. I hadn't been deaf to the subtle ways she would insult me, either, but now that Dan and I were divorced, all subtlety had dropped away. She had turned outright vicious.

This time in answer to my question rang out a regretful chorus of yeses. They did all know Dorothy.

It was time for me to take the leap. "Does anyone here know of a strawberry blonde woman who is a bit on the heavy side? Rachel might have been friends with her fiancé. They might have spent some time together." I hadn't meant to make any inferences by saying that the two had spent time together, but there were a lot of exchanged looks that hinted that I was referring to sexual impropriety. I was thankful I didn't need to spell it out.

"That Rachel would go after any man who looked at her twice," Paula said. "And if he was committed to somebody else, it was like she wanted him all the more. She didn't like it when someone had a toy she didn't have."

Everyone nodded agreement except for Rita. She seemed lost in thought. "Strawberry blonde..." she said as if thinking out loud. Then, she snapped her fingers. "I was at the hairdresser this past week and a woman came in to have her hair colored. I wouldn't have called it strawberry blonde at the time, but that's just what it was." She pulled her phone out of her purse. "I'll text my girl, Margot, and ask her if she knows the woman's name."

Two seconds later, Rita's phone sounded of wind chimes.

"Margot's going to text Janet and ask. That's the hairdresser that the woman was seeing."

I sat in amazement at this beautifully connected network that was taking shape right before my eyes. My heart pounded erratically in my chest as I waited for an answer to make its way back through Rita's phone. Meanwhile, the group returned to talking about the book and the injustice done to Tom Robinson, that man who had been wrongly accused in the book *To Kill a Mockingbird*. From the ladies' talk, I knew that there had been no justice for him. I could only hope that my outcome fared better.

I nearly jumped when the wind chimes sounded again.

Rita picked up her phone, read the message, and then held her phone up triumphantly. "Chloe Barns!"

"Ohhhh," Paula said and there were similar

sounds of recognition made by other women in the group. I glanced at Zoey, but she gave a little shake of her head. She didn't know a Chloe Barns either.

"I don't think that Chloe is seeing anybody right now," Rita said.

"She'd been dating Ned Mayes earlier in the year," Agatha said.

A few of the women grimaced, clearly not impressed with whoever Ned Mayes was.

The group's conversation shifted into other topics, starting at infidelity, going to honeymoons in Vegas and then to bacon. The transitions made sense at the time, but I couldn't have described how later.

Somehow the conversation came back around to Rachel.

"Let's face it, Veronica's better off without Rachel," said the woman with the round glasses and auburn hair. "Rachel was so spiteful and vindictive." Then to me, she said, "The only reason I don't think you killed her was because you didn't know her long enough. She was usually nice to people at first, would do anything for you and make you think she was your best friend."

"I heard that Veronica will inherit Rachel's side of their duplex," Paula said.

"Does that mean that Veronica and her family won't have to move?" Rita asked, sounding excited.

"No, they'll be able to rent out Rachel's side to cover their expenses," Paula answered.

It was during this quick exchange that it truly hit me for the first time. I was living in a small town. A small fishbowl of a town where everybody knew everybody else's business. I suddenly felt very exposed. But what left me feeling exposed could also be used to my advantage.

"Does anybody know anything about Ned Mayes?" I asked.

"He's nobody's loss," Rita answered. "Thinks he's more than he is." No one had anything more to add to that, and soon the ladies were talking about birthday cards and old family recipes for biscuits and cobblers.

I leaned closed to Zoey. "Do you know who Ned Mayes is?" I whispered.

"Nope, but I'm going to help you find out."

CHAPTER 18

*T*he next day, I left the café in Sam's capable hands and Zoey and I went to see Chloe. The day was cold and I had to wrap my waist-fitted princess coat around me. It was one of the few red garments I'd ever found that didn't clash with my red hair.

Everywhere else that I looked, people were wearing jackets or overcoats. Function definitely won over fashion, and I had to appreciate the warmth that some of the thickly padded coats provided.

Next to me, Zoey was sporting a lightweight olive green army jacket that hung a third of the way down her thighs. Under it she wore a hot pink thermal underwear shirt that hugged her every curve over a pair of black jeans and lace-up army boots. The girl looked ready to kick some heinie, which was a good thing. I hadn't thought through my choice of footwear and had donned a pair of flat Grecian-style sandals. I'd thought that they would be easy to walk in, but I hadn't factored in frozen toes.

Zoey led the way, and we walked three blocks up Main Street and then one street back. It had taken Zoey all of four minutes of snooping on Facebook to figure out that Chloe worked at Sew New, the local sewing and fabric store.

Warm air and a vanilla spice candle greeted us as soon as we stepped into the store. The floor was split up into three sections. The biggest section consisted of more fabric than I could have ever imagined could fit in such a compact space. The next section consisted of all the tools a person would need to work with the fabric. Then finally there was the checkout counter, behind which stood a plump woman with, you guessed it, strawberry blonde hair. And, just as Veronica had said, the woman was quite pretty.

On the woman's cardigan was a name tag. We'd found Chloe.

I had heard Veronica's account of what had happened between Rachel and Chloe. Now I needed to verify that information by hearing it from Chloe as well. Chloe was a murder suspect, pure and simple. Veronica was a murder suspect, too. Okay, sure, as far as I knew they weren't considered murder suspects by the police, but this was where my investigation had taken me, and I had to follow through with questioning my new suspect.

I swallowed. Hard. I was no longer feeling cold. I was burning hot. The pressure of asking all the right questions what were needed to clear my name weighed on me.

"Y'all let me know if you need anything," Chloe said with a bright smile before returning her attention to a stack of color swatches. She was thumbing through them and taking notes.

I wondered if we should shop first and then try to chat Chloe up as we checked out or if we should try talking to her now. I glanced around the store. It was empty, but the longer we were inside, the more likely another customer would come in and we would lose our opportunity for Chloe to candidly speak her mind... and hopefully tell the truth.

Giving Zoey a little nudge to alert her of my

intentions, I approached the counter behind which Chloe stood.

"Hi!" I said with more enthusiasm than I'd intended. I inwardly cringed but kept a smile plastered on my face. "We were hoping we could have a few minutes of your time."

Chloe looked up from her work and her face fell. "Ohhh, I'm so sorry. The owner doesn't allow proselytizing in the store, but if you have a pamphlet I'd be happy to take it and look it over later after I get off work." She gave a sympathetic but encouraging smile, and my heart melted. She was beyond nice! Back in Chicago, if people had come into our place of business to sell their brand of religion, I would have marched them right back outside and told them in no uncertain terms that if they ever came back that I'd call the cops.

There was no way she could have killed Rachel, because nice people didn't kill other people, right?

I had to give myself a mental slap. That way of thinking was full of bias and had absolutely no substance. Of course nice people could kill other people. If a nice person was pushed far enough, they could do just about anything, and that included hurting another person.

Zoey chimed in. "We actually wanted to talk to you about Ned."

Chloe's back stiffened and her expression turned placid. She would have made a great poker player. She wasn't giving anything away. "What about Ned?" Her voice was just as neutral as her face.

"It's a small town," I said apologetically. "I knew Rachel very briefly before she died, and her death has made something of an impression on me. I was hoping that by talking to the people who knew her that maybe I could understand what happened better." Okay, that wasn't exactly a fib.

Chloe's lips thinned. "Well, I can save you some time, because I didn't know her."

Zoey leaned forward with both hands on the counter, getting into Chloe's personal space. "But didn't you come to her house and scream at her in the middle of the night?"

This time Chloe's eyes narrowed. "What do you know about that?" Her words were clipped with barely concealed anger.

The change in her demeanor made me want to cheer. It meant we were getting somewhere.

"We spoke to Veronica, Rachel's sister," I said with calm slowness. I didn't want Chloe to get so upset that she refused to talk to us altogether. "She was next door the night that you went to Rachel's and warned her to stay away from your fiancé."

"Well if you know all that already, what do you need to talk to me for?" Chloe all but spat the words.

Zoey's shoulders went back and her chin lifted, going into fight mode. "Because we want to know if that's why you killed her."

"You what!" Chloe screeched.

"We just need to know enough to rule you out as a suspect," I rushed the words, getting them out as fast as I could before Chloe demanded that we leave the store. "And I didn't kill her either, but the police think I did... so that's why I'm here to talk to you. I'm trying to figure out who did kill her."

Chloe's brows were halfway up to her hairline, and she was looking at me as if I'd just sprouted a second head. Then to my shock and utter dismay, she slapped the counter and broke out in a bout of laughter that filled the store.

Zoey and I looked at each other, and Zoey shrugged her shoulders. Neither of us had a clue about Chloe's sudden change. Together, we returned our attention to Chloe.

"Ohhh," Chloe sighed, wiping laughter tears from the corners of her eyes. "That... that... that Jezebel did me the biggest favor of my life. She saved me from marrying Ned Mayes. I didn't want to see it at first, but he was mean. See, that's not how he started out. He was sweet to me early on when we first got together. I figured he'd be sweet again just as soon as we got past our wedding and were actually married, but he weren't ever gonna be sweet to me again. I was finally seeing the real him. The person he was when we first met, that was the fake him. I'd been convinced that it was the other way around, but after realizing he'd been carrying on with that hateful woman, I was finally able to see the truth." She looked us both right the in the eyes. "I know she weren't trying to do me any favors by sleepin' around with my fiancé, but she did. She saved me from a life-time of regret. Whoever killed her, I'm sure they had their reasons, but it wasn't me."

CHAPTER 19

We were doing way more walking than I'd ever expected today, and my poor toes were frozen by the time we reached the mechanic's garage on the far end of Main Street. Chloe had said that she'd gladly dumped Ned after his affair with Rachel, but I couldn't take her word for it. We had to hear what Ned said about the situation. While Chloe had seemed nice, it was possible she could actually be a femme fatale determined to destroy anyone who slipped out of her grasp.

"Hello?" I called out as I peeked around the edge of the white-painted cinderblock wall that made up the outer façade of the garage. The sound of metal clanking on metal stopped. I dared to step further into the garage, but as soon as I saw the man within, I was glad to have Zoey by my side.

Dressed in a grease-stained light blue mechanic's shirt overtop navy blue workman's slacks, a man who was almost as round as he was tall stepped out from behind the open hood of a car. "What can I do you for?" he asked, wiping his thick hands on a very dirty rag. While his voice sounded welcoming, his gray eyes were small and cold. As they scanned me from the top of my head to my feet and back up again, all I could think was that I would not want him to escort me home after a party on a late night. He gave me the creeps.

"Are you Ned?" I asked.

"Depends who's asking," he said with a smile that looked as greasy as his clothes. His teeth were stained an ugly yellow from what I assumed was a heavy smoker's habit.

Chloe was such a well put-together lady. I couldn't picture her with him, and I felt very sure that she was in fact better off without him. Her claim of having an epiphany that Ned was not a suitable match was so far holding up.

"We were hoping to talk to people who

knew Rachel Summers," Zoey said. "We've been asked to speak at her funeral, so we're going around talking with her friends to get some ideas of what to say."

Some of the smarminess of Ned's expression fell away. "Oh, yeah. Okay."

"And we were looking for Ned because we heard that they knew each other," I said. I was sure that this was Ned, but we needed the confirmation.

"Yeah, well, you found 'im," he said, tapping a name patch sewn into his shirt. It was blackened with so much grease I hadn't even noticed it. "Yeah, Rachel was a fine, upstanding woman in the community. She was always doing kind things and thinking of others. Never met a more generous person in my life. A lot of people are going to miss her."

So... Ned was a liar.

Zoey shoved her hands deep into her jacket's pockets. "We'd heard that you and Rachel were particularly close."

Ned's eyes darted back and forth between us, and then his smarmy smile returned. "Rachel was a very beautiful woman, and it's true that she enjoyed a man's company." His chest puffed up like a peacock's, but he wasn't anything near as pretty.

"Was it true that she enjoyed your 'company' while you were engaged to Chloe?" I asked.

His expression sobered. "That was a mistake, I admit it. I shouldn't have done that to Chloe, but Rachel made me see the light. I was about to marry down. Chloe's a nice girl and all, but I had to cut her loose. I've got a lot to offer a woman, if you know what I mean, and she fell short of the type of woman I deserve." He leered at me while he said it, looking me up and down with a smirk that pulled his mouth crooked.

I did my best to suppress an involuntary shiver of revulsion.

"So you dumped Chloe?" Zoey asked.

"Like a great big steaming turd," he said with pride and not an ounce of shame.

"She said she dumped you," I said.

Ned scowled. "This don't sound like stuff a person would say at a funeral." The statement was full of accusation.

"So, she did dump you?" I asked again, determined to stay on topic.

"No! I dumped her! Chloe's a hag. After Rachel, I knew I could do better than Chloe. I deserve someone like you, Red," he said, looking at me up and down again. "I could show you a real good time."

I momentarily choked on vomit, but Ned didn't seem to notice my distress. Instead, he kept on talking.

"I'd take you somewhere real nice for dinner, somewhere with waiters and waitresses and shit. By the end of the night, I'd make you happy to be a woman."

"Okay!" I held up my hands, palms out, hoping that would make him stop. "Chloe, did she try to get back together with you? Did she get mad or anything?"

Ned's eyes widened. "Oh yeah! She begged. Cried like a baby. Said she'd do anything just as long as I didn't leave her 'cause she knew she'd never do better than me." He was smiling and his chest was pumped up big again.

We'd already established that Ned was a liar when he'd said that Rachel was well regarded within the community. It didn't take too far of a stretch in reasoning to conclude that he was lying about Chloe, too. At the very least, I figured that Chloe and Ned's break up was mutual.

"I wasn't kidding about taking you out,"

Ned said, sidling up closer to me. He smelled so strongly of oil and gasoline that I would have been concerned for his safety if someone were nearby smoking.

"Thank you for the invitation, but—"

"Now, come on, give a fella a chance." He winked. "Tell you what. I'm part of a walking group that's been put together by Joel Mullen."

"Joel... the guy at the newspaper?"

"Joel, the guy who *owns* the newspaper," Ned corrected with a twinkle in his eye, and I got the impression that he was trying to name drop in hopes that it would add to his personal clout. "Me and him, we're real tight. Why don't you come along? We walk every Saturday. We used to stop for coffee and cake at Sarah's Eatery afterward, but since it got bought out, it's turned into a dump and we don't stop there no more."

My mouth gaped at him.

"Wha? What I say?" Ned looked from me to Zoey and back again.

"I'm the new owner of Sarah's Eatery!"

"You're that dumb northerner who keeps givin' everybody food poisoning?"

I could feel my blood pressure rising. "No, I haven't given anyone food poisoning. Ever!"

Ned didn't look convinced. "Well, that don't mean the food's any good. I heard it's all cookies from the grocery store. If I want cookies from the grocery store, I can go buy them from the grocery store!"

My cheeks flamed. It was one thing to be told the truth about yourself by someone you thought well of, but it was completely something else to be told the truth about yourself by someone you equated to a slug living under a rock a few feet off of a cesspool.

"Well... well..." I spluttered, so upset and embarrassed that I was having trouble putting words together. "I'm going to talk to Joel. The walking group *will* come to the café after your walk, and you *will* have coffee and dessert. On the house!"

"I don't know." I saw fear flash in his eyes. "Dorothy's not gonna like that."

That was it. There was going to be another murder in this town, and it would be one that I actually committed. I was going to bake a cake and shove it down Dorothy's throat until she choked on it.

CHAPTER 20

*W*ith the adventure of the day complete, Sage and I retired to the empty apartment upstairs and I lay on my floor mattress and wondered what to do to turn things around for the café. If it weren't for the rent I'd gotten from the other businesses on my block, I wouldn't have even been able to afford the cookies I'd been getting from the grocery store.

Life felt bleak. It felt awful. The café was failing, and I couldn't do very much about it until after I cleared my name. It sort of put a damper on people's appetites when they thought that what you were serving them might come with a side of strychnine.

I scowled into the darkness, angry at everything, but then a little fur ball of love snuggled up against me and started purring.

"You're the best, Sage." I gave her a little tickle behind her ear. She sneezed and I remembered that I still hadn't taken her to the vet. "I'm sorry, little girl. I'm going to get on that real soon. We'll get you all doctored up so that you can be my buddy for a long, long time."

I drifted off to sleep with a smile on my face and feeling much less alone in the world.

THE NEXT MORNING Joel walked into the café for the first time since Sarah had left. It should have made me want to do a happy dance, but instead I had to resist the urge to climb on top of the counter so that I could reach his too-tall neck and strangle him.

"Hey!" Jack said, flipping his ever-present newspaper to the side so that he could see what I was doing. What I was doing was overflowing his coffee cup. Thankfully, the saucer below had caught all of the overflow and none of it had dribbled off the side of the counter and onto Jack's fancy suit.

As quick as lightning, I got a clean, dry

saucer to replace the coffee-filled one and poured some of his filled-to-the-brim coffee out of his cup into an empty cup.

The mistake took some of the vinegar out of me, so I only mildly glared at Joel instead of having an all-consuming desire to tear his head off.

"I'll have an order of biscuits and gravy," Joel said as he sat down on the stool next to Jack. His shoulders took up all of his space and some of Jack's personal space, too.

Jack flipped one corner of his newspaper down so that he could peer speculatively at Joel. Jack and I both knew that Joel wouldn't be getting biscuits and gravy, and if Joel had bothered to be around since I'd taken over the café, he'd have known it too. With arched brows and a twinkle of amusement in Jack's eye, he quietly went back to reading.

"Sure! I'll be right back." My tone and smile was all saccharine as I headed into the back kitchen. I reappeared a few minutes later with a bowl of Brenda's spaghetti and meatballs that I'd heated up in a microwave. "Here you go," I said, putting the large bowl down in front of Joel. "Biscuits and gravy."

Jack chuckled, but his newspaper stayed in place.

Joel looked at the bowl in front of him and then up at me. "No chef yet?"

"You know how it is. With the loss of support from your Saturday walking group, hiring a chef had to be pushed down the list." I was so mad. He'd been one of Sarah's regulars. He'd supported her, and all of her other regulars had been incredibly supportive of me. Everyone but him. I'd thought that he was a nice guy, but now I wasn't so sure.

"Oh, sorry. I got outvoted." He twirled spaghetti around his fork and took a bite.

He'd gotten outvoted... If the walking club hadn't been coming for their after-walk coffee and cake and he'd been outvoted, that meant that he had wanted the group to continue to come to the café after their walks.

That did make me feel better. A little.

"So you're not against the group coming here after the walk?"

"Nope." He took another bite.

"Then how do I get them to come?"

"Come on the walk." He said it like it was the most obvious answer in the world.

I rolled my eyes. Joel was the second man to

try to talk me into joining the walking group, but I had better things to do. I had a killer to catch!

Joel put down his fork. "Community is important in small towns. Who you know and who said what is also important. Come on the walk and be a part of the community. Show everyone firsthand how great you are. Don't give them the chance to only take Dorothy's word about what you're like."

Conflicting emotions surged through me. He'd said I was great, but in the same breath he'd also mentioned my arch nemesis, my ex-aunt-in-law Dorothy. Both elation and rage surged through me at the same time. I did my best to fuel the happiness and put out the rampant fire of my rage.

But Joel wasn't done. He had one more carrot to hang in front of me.

"Rachel used to come on the walks." The spark in his eye told me that he knew how relevant that was. "You could talk to the people who knew her."

I felt like palming my forehead. *Of course* Rachel was connected to the walking group! She had been having an affair with Ned, and Ned was a member of the group. I couldn't believe I hadn't picked up on that possibility. If I went on the walk with the group, that would be that many more people who knew Rachel. It would be that many more people who Rachel could have screwed over. If nothing else, one of them could provide me with a clue I needed to figure out who to investigate next.

"I'll do it." Today was Thursday. That gave me two days to figure out what to serve the walking group when I forced them to reinstate their routine of finishing the walk at my café.

CHAPTER 21

*T*hursday had come and gone in a blur. I still didn't know what I was going to serve the walking group, but I had managed to make a vet appointment for little Miss Sage for Friday morning, which it now was.

"Thanks, Zoey," I said as I stepped out of the café's front door while Zoey held it open for me. She was on her way in, and her honey-tinted skin absolutely glowed in the soft morning light. Today she had Cleopatra eyes instead of cat eyes, and the double-winged flare at the corner of her almond-shaped eyes looked amazing.

Sage roamed around from one side to the

other within her hard-shell carrying crate, making it jiggle unsteadily in my hands. She meowed, and it was full of pitiful complaint.

"Taking her to the vet," I said to Zoey.

"Are you walking?"

"No, I was afraid my shoulder would break off after carrying this crate for more than a mile. Plus, it wouldn't be fair to Sage to get bounced around the whole time. I called an Uber." I was staying aware of traffic on the street as we talked so that I could see if my ride pulled up, but everything was moving slow. A huge SUV with heavily tinted windows was passing by at a snail's crawl, but when it got twenty feet past where we stood, it revved its engine and zoomed into a parallel spot across the street next to the sidewalk. It had dove into the spot with such a sudden burst of speed that its brakes screeched when the huge, heavy vehicle was slammed to a halt.

"Wow, somebody needs to go back to Driving 101," Zoey said, craning her neck to see over her shoulder.

"Do you get the feeling that they're looking at us?" I thought I could make out a little bit of movement behind the midnight dark windows, but I was pretty sure that was my imagination playing tricks on me.

"Totally." Zoey leaned this way and that, as if trying to find an angle that would allow her a glimpse inside. She looked back at me. "How's your investigation going?"

"Nowhere, but maybe it's going better than I thought." The SUV was giving me the heebie-jeebies. It was behaving so oddly in comparison to all the other traffic around us.

"You could have rattled the killer. Maybe they don't like you snooping." Zoey looked at the SUV again and then back at me. "Let's go rattle them some more." Her smile was luminous. It might have been the first time that I'd seen her without even a hint of sadness.

I didn't know how smart it was to go knock on the window of someone who had already arranged for one person to be put six feet in the ground, but if it made Zoey happy, that was a good enough reason for me.

I put Sage's crate down next to the café door. If we were heading into danger, she was better off staying behind.

Timing it just right so as not to get hit by the oncoming traffic, we jogged straight across the road to the sidewalk. Then, we made a beeline for the SUV. There was no point in sneaking. If the person inside was watching us, they already knew that we were heading toward them. Still yet, it was hard not to crouch or walk stealthier as we got closer.

Zoey giggled as we neared the passenger side door. She was having fun. I felt like I was having a heart attack.

"Noooo," I whisper hissed as Zoey's hand reached for the SUV's passenger side door handle. "They could have a gun!"

"And you think that leaving the door closed will protect us anymore?"

She had a good point. I shrugged my shoulders and motioned for her to go for it.

Her fingers slipped under the door's handle to open it, and the door's locks clicked home. She pulled on the door handle but the door didn't open.

Going for broke, I stepped up next to Zoey and wrapped on the passenger door's window with my knuckles before twirling my finger to indicate that I wanted whoever was inside to roll the window down.

The SUV's engine revved.

"You got your phone? You could take a picture of the car and the plates. Maybe you could find something out by doing one of your fancy searches on your computer."

"Oh yeah!" Zoey whipped out her phone, took a picture of the SUV from the side and then headed around to the back to get a picture of its plates. But she didn't get there in time.

The SUV lurched forward into a cacophony of honking horns. Tires screeched, and one of the cars made a hard right turn onto the sidewalk straight toward Zoey and me in an effort to avoid a collision with the SUV. I threw myself in one direction and Zoey threw herself in the other. When the car came to a halt and its door opened, a little woman who looked as though she had to be somebody's grandma got out of her car and shook her fist in the air at the hastily retreating SUV.

It wasn't even 8 AM yet.

CHAPTER 22

*S*itting in the vet's office thirty minutes later, I still felt a little shaken about having had a Mazda XXX almost crush me into a huevos rancheros-topped pancake.

Sage's hawk-like claws reached through the grate-style door of her carrier and hooked the sleeve of my coat. I let her pull my arm against the door and she rubbed her cheek against the crisscrossed steel just as if she were rubbing it directly on my arm.

"Sorry, girl. I'll get you out soon." I eyeballed the dog sitting a few feet away from us. It looked as though it was a cross between a bulldog and a moose. It was huge, and it hadn't taken its gaze off of Sage's carrier since the moment we sat down.

"Kylie Berry," the receptionist at the check-in counter called out.

"Here." I raised my hand to help her find me.

"Room three. The doctor will be with you soon."

I stood, picked up the carrier, waved goodbye to moose-dog and followed a hallway until I found room three. The door was open. I went in, closed the door, and opened the crate. Sage thanked me for her freedom by climbing up my body to my shoulder and then doing her best to climb on top of my head. I guessed that these vet trips were not going to be a favorite activity of hers.

On the other side of the room was another door, and I heard shuffling and murmured voices before the door opened. A slender man in his mid-thirties or early forties walked in. He was very fit, and somewhat handsome with salt and pepper hair. He smile was warm, and I felt instantly at ease. I couldn't say the same for Sage, though. She had her two front paws on top of my head and one of her back paws trying to fit itself in my ear to use it as a stepping stool.

"Who do we have here?" the doctor asked.

"I'm Kylie, and this is Sage." I reached up to picking Sage up from my head, but she dug her claws into my scalp. The doctor stepped in to help. Sage hissed, I screeched, and my hair turned into Sage's last hopes for staying in place. In the end, she lost the battle… and so did my hair.

"Well hello, Sage," the doctor said with the kitten now standing on a stainless steel table. "I'm Dr. Doogan." Then to me, he asked, "Did anything specific bring you in today?"

"No, I found her one day when I went for a walk. Someone nearby said she was a stray and that nobody wanted her, so I took her home with me."

The doctor *tsk*ed. "I'm glad you two found each other."

"She sneezed a couple of days ago."

"Oh! Well let's take a listen." He pulled out his stethoscope and put it to her chest, but that was exactly the moment that Sage chose to start purring very loudly. It didn't seem to bother the doctor, though. "I don't think I've seen you here before," he said once he was done listening.

"I'm new in town. I'm the new owner of Sarah's Eatery."

"Oh! Congratulations."

I was pretty sure that that meant that he hadn't heard anything about me. That was a major plus, because it also meant that my ex-aunt-in-law hadn't turned him against me. "I've actually been investigating the recent murder of Rachel Summers. Did you know her, I mean, did she have a pet?"

The doc shone a light in both of Sage's eyes. "Hm, I did have the misfortune of having met Rachel Summers. She got a kitten from the local shelter and brought him in for a wellness checkup, but she spent the whole visit trying to get me to go out to dinner with her. As you can imagine, that wouldn't have gone over very well with my husband. I heard that she returned the kitten to the shelter the very next day."

I had just learned a whole lot, and I blinked a couple of times to absorb it all. "If you're married to a man, why did Rachel try to get you to go out to dinner with her?"

"I don't know, but she got mad when she didn't get her way. Stormed out without the kitten, then came back a few minutes later...

Terrible woman. Nasty piece of work." The doc pushed the tip of a thermometer into a spot that Sage had some negative feelings about as well. "I could tell you all kinds of stories on her. She poisoned a dog—" I gasped, "—which with some help had a tummy ache but otherwise was fine. She campaigned to have the animal shelter shut down on the grounds that it was 'unsightly.' She came in to ask me what it would take to raise foxes because she wanted to have them made into a fox fur coat. And she is believed to have stolen money from a fundraiser to cover the expense of spays and neuters for the town residents."

I couldn't believe what I was hearing. I felt like I needed to sit down. I'd heard a lot of people say unflattering things about Rachel, but no one had been able to sum up quite so succinctly what a terrible person she really had been.

And I had *hired* her!

Knowing that made me feel nauseous, and what did it say about my ability to read a person's character? Of course, I'd married my no good, selfish, self-centered, cheating husband, so I guess my inability to read a person's character shouldn't have surprised me quite so much.

I watched as Dr. Doogan gave Sage one shot and then another. Sage didn't even complain. She was so brave.

"Am… am I doing things right? With her? I've never had a pet before."

Dr. Doogan's head shot up. His eyes were wide. "Not even as a kid?" He sounded dismayed, and I felt like a cretin.

I shook my head, and he *tsk*ed. Giving Sage his full attention, he said, "Water, food, sunshine, fresh air, love and play. Give your kitten these things, and you'll both be just fine. The receptionist can give you a list of recommended pet food brands."

CHAPTER 23

*L*ying in bed that night with Sage curled up sleeping on my stomach, the vet's reaction to me never having had a pet before still stung. When I was a kid, I hadn't had any choice in the matter. It had been my parents' choice not to have pets because my mom struggled with allergies. But then I'd gotten married and moved away. Why hadn't I gotten a pet then?

There was the Christmas that I'd thought Dan had gotten me a puppy, but it turned out to be surprise tickets to a hot new play. Front row seats. I later found out that his then-girlfriend had been starring in it. That had explained his forty-five minute trip to the "bathroom" as soon as the play had ended. He'd gone backstage to spend time with her.

So much about Dan and who he was had come out during the divorce, but I was beginning to realize that I still had a lot to learn about myself. For the first eighteen years of my life, I had been my parents' child. Then, the next eleven years of my life had been spent as Dan's wife. I had never lived a life of my own making before, but I was glad it was happening now. It was overdue.

I looked down at Sage as she shifted and then purred. I gave her nose a little rub and she purred louder, but she lifted her head up suddenly, full of alertness, when an unfamiliar sound reached our ears. It was there one moment and gone the next. It sounded like an attempt to move something that was stuck.

Sage and I remained completely silent. Then, we heard it again. Shock and fear shot through my veins. The sound was coming from the hallway outside my open bedroom door!

Displacing Sage, I got to my feet and tiptoed across the cold hardwood floor wearing nothing but a long t-shirt. Stopping at the door, I leaned my head into the hallway and looked this way and that. I gasped and jerked my head back into the bedroom when I spotted a shadow moving beyond the window at the end of the hall. It was the window that overlooked the building's back parking lot.

I held my breath to try to keep from hyperventilating and stuck my head back out into the hallway. Sage chose that exact moment to go bounding into the hallway, hissing and spitting as she hopped on straight legs. Her fur was sticking straight out from her body, making her look like a cross between a porcupine and a fuzzball.

"Sage!" It was a whisper, but it was the loudest whisper I'd ever heard. It filled the space around us and bounced off the walls. I made a mad dash into the hallway to scoop Sage into my arms, and then stood frozen as a death-like shadow loomed in the window at the end of the hall. I was too afraid to scream.

The shadow moved, the window jiggled, and Sage launched herself from my arms and threw herself full bodied against the window before dropping to the floor to try all over again.

When Sage hit the window, the shadow jerked back, and I found my voice. I screamed. I screamed so loud that I was sure that plaster was cracking and glasses were breaking somewhere.

The shadow disappeared and the clang of hard footfalls on the metal fire escape outside was all that remained.

Dashing back inside the bedroom, I scrambled in the dark to find my cell phone. I dialed 9-1-1.

"State the nature of your emergency," an operator said.

"*Someonestryingtobreakin!* I live above Sarah's Eatery."

"I'm sorry. Can you repeat that? Please talk slower."

"Brad. Brad Calderos. Is he there? Can I speak to him?" I held my hand against my chest as hard as I could to keep my heart from breaking its way out of my chest.

"Officer Claderos is on another call and is currently unavailable. Please state the nature of your emergency."

Sage strolled back into the bedroom. She sat down, lifted her leg and started grooming herself. The bad guy was gone, and she was back to being totally chill... And I was being an overreacting ninny.

"Never mind... never mind. Everything's

fine," I assured the operator. Tomorrow I would put a motion detection light outside the window or do something else similar. I imagined how pretty Christmas lights would be strewn all around it. That would be cheap and easy to set up, and it would provide good illumination. No more shadow people for me. Besides that, whoever it was had been scared off by a kitten. If they got scared away by a kitten, I was pretty sure that I was going to be okay.

I DIDN'T KNOW how much time had passed when I heard the disembodied sound of a man's voice invade my dreams. I went from being completely asleep to fully awake with no transition in-between.

"Hello?" a man's voice called out again, and it was not muted by any walls, glass, or even curtains.

Someone was in the apartment!

I jumped to my feet. It was dark, but I could tell that my protector cat wasn't anywhere around me.

Glancing frantically around my bedroom, I

looked for something that I could use as a weapon.

Mattress? No.

The dress I use as a blanket? No.

My phone? Yes! I could throw it at his head. Why I thought of throwing it at his head instead of using it to call for help, I don't know. All I knew was that there was a man in my apartment, uninvited, and the sound of his footfalls meant that he was walking down the hall toward my bedroom.

Standing up, I tiptoed to stand behind my bedroom door, and I waited.

"Hello?" The voice was so close. The hairs on my arms lifted.

An arm extended past the door, then a shoulder, then his head.

I struck! Holding my cell phone like a spike, I drove it down on top of the intruder's head.

Instead of crying out or jerking away, the man's arm whipped around. His big hand wrapped around my wrist, taking control of my arm, and then his other hand pressed into my shoulder to push me face-first against the door.

"Kylie?"

Twisting my neck, I looked behind me.

Relief flooded all my senses. "Brad!" As always, he looked good in his officer's uniform.

Brad released me, and I rubbed my now sore wrist.

"What are you doing here? And how did you get in here?"

Brad walked over to the light switch and turned it on. It wasn't until that moment that I remembered that I was only wearing a long t-shirt that fell down my legs as far as the shortest of miniskirts.

Brad didn't seem to take notice of this, and I wasn't sure which to be more upset about—the fact that he was in my home in the middle of the night uninvited or that he was completely unaffected by the sight of me.

"How did you get in?" I asked again. This time I let my fear shift into anger.

"Sarah gave me a key."

"Do I look like Sarah?"

He had the nerve to look me up and down. The corner of his mouth quirked up and one of his cheeks dimpled. "Nope."

Ohhhh, I wanted to hit him. "Give me the key." I held out my palm.

"Nope." He strolled out of the bedroom and continued to look around the apartment.

"Why'd you call the station? Sally in Dispatch told me she'd gotten a call."

I followed him out into the hallway. "Someone tried to break in."

He twisted at the waist to turn and look at me, one brow lifted. For the first time, I saw actual concern in his eyes. "Where'd they try to break in from?"

I pointed toward the window at the end of the hall.

Walking with purpose instead of strolling, Brad approached the window and tried to open it. "Painted shut. You need to fix that. Your fire escape is out this window. You need to be able to leave through it."

Duh. I didn't say it, but I wanted to.

Brad turned around and looked at me. "This needs to get fixed." He was dead serious.

"Okay, okay... I'll get it fixed."

He nodded, then shown his flashlight out the window and traced the fire escape with its beam.

"You going to check for fingerprints?"

"They were most likely wearing gloves. Things don't work like *CSI* or one of those other shows, Kylie."

My anger spiked again. This was the second

time he'd chastised me in my own home—a home that he'd broken into.

"I didn't kill Rachel." I spat the words.

Brad clicked the flashlight off and turned around. "Did say you did."

My mouth gaped. "What about the big search you did?"

"Due diligence. Had to do things right so that there wouldn't be questions about it later."

I didn't know what to say. It was kind of sounding like he'd actually been trying to protect me.

"Word is you've been asking questions around town about Rachel."

Okay, so that came out of left field.

"So," I said, feeling more than a little bit defiant.

"So you need to stop."

"Nope."

This time both sides of his mouth quirked up.

"Why didn't you tell me that the brownies she'd been eating weren't burnt?" I asked.

"You are not a member of this investigation."

"What's that got to do with anything?"

"Meaning… it's none of your business."

Heat flamed my cheeks and my hands balled into fists. "Accused of murder. A café that is circling the drain. And my previously non-existent reputation setting me up to be a modern-day re-telling of *Arsenic and Old Lace*. None of my business?" I was yelling by the end of what I'd had to say.

"Stop asking questions about Rachel, Kylie. Let the professionals"—he tapped his chest —"handle this."

CHAPTER 24

*I*t was the next day, and I was in the grocery store. I'd left Brenda in charge of the café while I checked the deli for anything marked on sale. There was a carrot cake marked down to seventeen dollars. The original price had been twenty-five. All I could do was stand and shake my head. It wasn't even a very big cake. Best I could figure is that the carrots used in the cake had been grown in gold-laced soil.

I put the carrot cake back and picked out an assortment of three dozen cookies and a German chocolate cake. It didn't matter to me that the cake was priced to move and was therefore probably already considered a little old. It wasn't gonna get much older. Whatever slices didn't sell at the café today were going to go upstairs to the apartment with me tonight. I figured that I could put one slice under the window leading out to the fire escape. If someone tried to break in, maybe they'd slip on it and make a lot of noise, giving me a chance to escape or hit them with the pointy end of one of my high heel shoes.

As for the other pieces of cake, I'd call them dinner. I couldn't wait. I was already dreaming of the great big, tall glass of ice cold milk that I was going to have with it.

"Oh, hey… sorry," I said when my food laden daydream let me step right into the path of a man trying to get by me.

"No problem," he said with a half turn as he walked on, but that was all it took.

That profile… That hair… Those shoulders. It was Max! Zoey's Max! The ghost turned flesh. And he was right here walking around Camden Falls' grocery store with an arm basket of oranges, nuts, and avocados. I didn't know what to be more upset about, the fact that the man who had ripped Zoey's heart out of her chest was walking around Camden Falls like he hadn't been missing or that his basket of food was so disgustingly healthy that it made me feel guilty about my own dinner plans.

I turned my buggy the opposite direction and pushed, digging my cell phone out of my purse as I zigzagged through customers. I hit dial and it rang. Then rang. Then rang. Nothing.

I swore under my breath, reached the end of the aisle and stopped, searching behind me for Max.

No Max.

I headed to the next aisle and the next aisle.

No Max.

I went to the front of the store. The check-out lanes had a few people in them... but no Max.

My stomach fell with the feeling of having had a heavy rock dropped in it. I didn't want to tell Zoey who I'd just seen. I wanted to protect her from hearing that her ghosting ex was back, but knowing Zoey and all of the surveillance access she had, there was a really good chance I wouldn't have to tell her a thing. There was a really good chance she already knew.

$\mathcal{I}$ spent the rest of the day and half the night worrying about Zoey. I tried calling her three more times, and each time I almost left her a message telling her the unthinkable—that Max was back in town—but I couldn't bring myself to leave that kind of news on her voicemail. I finally gave up and went to sleep, drunk on chocolate cake and ice-cold milk.

The next day was Saturday, and the walking group was meeting at 9 AM in a small park a couple of blocks over and one road down. I squeezed myself into a pair of skin-tight yoga pants and then covered my cake belly with a tee. After pulling my flaming red locks into a ponytail, I was ready to go.

I was huffing by the time I finished my speed walk from the café to the park, and I slowed down once I had it in sight so that no one would see me struggling to catch my breath. It was one thing to go for a walk. It was something entirely different to look like you needed the exercise of going for a walk.

Spotting Joel spotting me, I waved and strolled over to where the group was gathered. There was a couple with an eager and alert border collie, a laid-back fellow with a flat faced pug with huge puppy-dog eyes, a silver-haired couple in matching blue tracksuits, and Ned. Ned was cleaned up and out of his grease-stained uniform from the service garage, but I couldn't say more than that about any improvements. His teeth were still stained a smoker's yellow, and what little hair he had looked as though it had spent three hours working over a deep fryer just this morning alone. Why Rachel had had an affair with him, I'd never understand.

"Glad to see everybody," Joel said, and it had the same effect as calling everyone to attention. All eyes were on him, and he stood like a larger-than-life statue in the center of the group. "This here's Kylie Berry, and she'll be joining us this morning."

"And there's coffee and cookies waiting for us at the café—on the house—at the end of the walk," I quickly chimed in with as much enthusiasm as I could muster without actually breaking into a cheer.

Everyone around me, minus Joel, looked at each other but not at me. They said nothing to confirm a willingness to go to the café after the walk.

It was the definition of awkward, but then the pug sneezed and the group took the opportunity to *ooh* and *awww* over his sniffles before heading out. Joel tossed me a shoulder shrug as if to say he'd tried and then fell in with the group. I quickly caught up with him.

"Hey, thanks for inviting me on the walk. I thought about it and you're right, I need to do more to become a part of the community."

"And maybe learning how to cook wouldn't hurt either." He gave me a little elbow nudge on my shoulder as if to soften the truth of his words.

I balanced my palms in front of me, pretending they were scales. "Learn how to cook... Stay out of jail... A girl's gotta have her priorities." I had to crane my neck way back to give him a smile and a wink. He rewarded me with a smile back, and just like all the other times he'd smiled, he went from boyishly charming to disarmingly handsome. The transformation left me spellbound every time.

To save me from embarrassing myself by staring too long into his warm brown eyes, I turned my attention to the group in front of us. "Who should I talk to first?"

"Hmmm, Adam—the guy with the pug—is the person who introduced Rachel to the group a couple of years ago. You might start with him."

"Got it." I went into power-walk mode, swinging my hips and pumping my arms, to catch up with Adam. His little pug was prancing next to him, making occasional snort-snort sounds that made me want to wrap the little guy in my arms like a baby and use a suction bulb on his sinuses to open them up. "Cute dog!" I exclaimed as an icebreaker.

"Thanks." He looked me up and down, assessing me, and then I could see the shift in his eyes. He'd decided to like me. "So you took over Sarah's Eatery? Dorothy Hibbert has sure had a lot to say about that."

I cringed. "She's my ex-aunt-in-law. I think she has a for-reals crush on my ex-husband and she never considered me good enough."

Adam looked at me sharply and I realized what I'd said. I had just claimed that Dorothy Hibbert, a supposed pillar in the community— or at least a bully—had had a raging crush on her nephew. I immediately wanted to take the words back. That is, until Adam smirked and chuckled. "Yeah, I've always thought that one was wound a bit tight. She always seems so sure of how everybody else is so wrong."

Instantly I felt as though I'd made a new friend, but now I had to hit the thin shell of our fledgling friendship with an ice pick. "I'm awfully sorry about what happened to Rachel. Joel said that you two had known each other."

"Oh yeah, Rach and me were a thing for about a year." He nodded his head and the focus of his eyes drifted as if remembering.

"Good times?"

He did a one-sided shoulder head nod. "Sometimes." Pause. "Did you know her?"

"Very briefly. Actually, I hired her. She was going to work at the café." I didn't mention that I'd hired her as a chef given that she didn't know how to cook. I really had to rethink some of my business decisions regarding the café. In retrospect, hiring her was like I was begging the universe to let me fail. "She died before she ever started working. It really left me feeling like there's this big question mark where she was. I was all set to get to know her, and then she was taken away." I was avoiding saying the word "murdered" in case news had traveled about me being prime suspect number one.

"Didn't you bake the brownies she was eating when she died?"

Sugar snaps! "Maybe not those exact brownies…" The conversation lagged, and when I spoke again, I made sure to bring it back to Rachel and not what might have killed her, that is to say… me. "Were you two pretty serious?"

"Mmm, more fun than serious. Well, fun some of the times. She'd run a bit hot and cold on me. We were on and off for the better part of a year. By the time it ended, I was honestly already over the whole thing." He added quickly, "I am sorry she died, though."

I think that he might have been the first person to have said so.

"Was Rachel close with anyone else in the walking group?"

Adam didn't need a second to ponder. He answered right away. "She and Jerry walked together a lot."

I scanned the group, wondering which one Jerry was. It wasn't lost on me that Rachel was being connected with yet another man and not a woman. There was a definite trend to her ways.

"Jerry and Michelle, his wife, have the border collie."

I instantly had a sinking feeling. Jerry was handsome and unavailable, the latter making him exactly Rachel's type. I watched as the fluffy-haired black and white dog pranced around the couple. He wasn't on a leash but he stayed near his human parents anyway. They clearly doted on him, and he on them.

Jerry pulled a ball out of his pocket and threw it into a house's unfenced yard. The dog went full tilt running after it, and Michelle met the dog on her knees and with open arms when he brought the ball back. She then got to her feet and bent over the dog while it spun in circles, overjoyed with the one-on-one attention.

Jerry continued to walk as Michelle ran past, he blond curls bouncing as she ran. She was waving the ball over her head as the dog did hind-legged pogo hops to chase after her.

I quickened my pace and slid into position next to Jerry. Glancing up at him, I realized he really was very handsome. He was car-salesman handsome. He had a bright smile and an easy charisma that would make him the center of the universe at any party.

"Hi, that's a beautiful dog you have." Since the line had worked so well with Adam, I decided to use it again with Jerry.

"Thanks." He gave me a not-unfriendly smile, but he didn't say anything more. It was going to be up to me to build some momentum into our conversation.

"Have you had him long?"

"My wife already had him when we first got together about four years back."

"You two haven't been married long?"

"Three years."

"Congratulations!"

"Thanks," he said, this time with a thinness to his lips.

"Marriage is a lot of work."

"Yep."

"I guess someone like Rachel has a way of making it even harder."

Jerry shot me a look, and his jaw was clenched tight.

"How long were you two having an affair?" It was a shot in the dark, and I held my breath waiting to see if it would hit.

"That was a long time ago." The words were said so low, almost under his breath, that I barely heard them. "My wife and I are in a good place now, and it's none of your business, so why don't you leave it alone?"

But I couldn't leave it alone. Someone had wanted Rachel dead, and I needed to know who. "How long were you together? When did it end?"

"I told you it's none of your business." His voice was low in an exaggerated way, and he barely moved his lips. He didn't want anyone to overhear. He didn't want his *wife* to overhear, and his wife was near. I had him at a disadvantage, leverage to keep him talking to me.

"I need to know," I pushed.

Jerry sighed, then looked at me and then to his wife. She was still playing with their dog.

"She doesn't know?"

"She knows." His voice was resigned.

"Rachel and me, it was a mistake. Michelle and I are working it out. Going to therapy. We're doing okay now."

"How long's it been since things ended?"

"About eight months."

"How long were you and Rachel together?"

"Close to a year."

"Why'd it end?"

"Michelle found out."

Ouch. "And she didn't leave you?"

Jerry shook his head, his gaze soft as he watched his wife. "She gave me a second chance. I should have never cheated. Rachel was just so…" He sighed heavily.

"Jus so… ?"

He grimaced. "Insistent. She made the grass look greener, if you know what I mean. She convinced me that I was disposable to Michelle… or that it didn't really matter. I don't know. Her reasoning always seemed to change. I think it boiled down to that she seemed fun and… Michelle had become less fun. It's like you said, marriage is work. I got tired of the work. I missed the play, and Rachel was a chance to play."

His honesty was like a hand reaching into my stomach and twisting everything around. I thought about Dan, my ex, and how he'd had his many, many, many playmates. I thought of all the times I'd wanted us to recapture the fun of our relationship by escaping for a long weekend away from the business or family. He'd always chide me and tell me I was being selfish.

Then I thought about Michelle's choice to forgive Jerry. Could she really have forgiven him? By the time the layers of lies had been stripped away to reveal the truth, I had been beyond done with Dan. Of course, Dan had had no intentions of changing. Maybe that was the difference between Dan and Jerry. Jerry had realized that the most important person to him was Michelle. To Dan, I was a cog in the machine of his life, nothing more.

"We're trying to have a baby." Jerry's words cut through my thoughts and they centered me like almost nothing else could.

"A baby?"

"Mmhmm," he said with a little grin pulling at his lips. His eyes had softened again, and he looked happy.

Maybe Michelle had forgiven him. He saw a future with her that extended beyond what either one of them could achieve alone.

"Did Rachel ever try to get back together with you after you ended things?"

That got his attention. "Yeah, a bunch of times. But I was done. The further away from her I got, the more I realized how much she'd twisted my thinking." He looked at me. "Make no mistake, what I did was wrong and the only person I can blame at the end of the day is me, but... she got in my head. Once I got her out, I wanted her to stay out."

"And Michelle, did she ever have anything to say to Rachel?"

"Michelle's a good woman, better than I deserve. She just wanted to move forward. We had some issues to work out, stuff that didn't even have anything to do with Rachel. 'Rachel was a symptom,' that's what Michelle says." He shrugged. "Like I said, she's better than me. She wasn't looking forward to being friends with Rachel, but she didn't kill her either." He looked at me, pointedly. "She didn't bake those brownies."

CHAPTER 26

I dropped back in the group to walk next to Joel. I needed to lick my wounds a little bit after Jerry's brownies comment. Seeing the belief in his eyes that I had killed Rachel had unnerved me to my core. But could I blame him? Even I thought that I was a terrible cook. When the police had brought that box of rat poison out from the pantry, I'd thought that I'd mixed up the ingredients and had killed her. It wasn't until I'd heard Veronica say the brownies were perfectly cooked—not burnt—that I'd known that someone else had been involved in Rachel's demise. It hadn't been me.

"Not going so well?" Joel asked. His hands

were shoved deep into his pants pockets and he lumbered along with one step to my two.

"It's going great." I said it, and I meant it. I was learning so much, but that didn't stop me from feeling like the slimy stuff a person finds under a rock they've pulled out of a pond. "I need to talk to Michelle next."

We walked a little in quiet before Joel spoke again. "What you waitin' for?"

I didn't know the answer to that. Facing Jerry's infidelity—and their saved marriage— made me feel like a lesser creature in comparison to his perfect wife, Michelle. She'd fought to save her marriage. I'd given up and had run away. That couldn't be how it had happened. It couldn't be all there was to it, yet they were together and I was facing life's struggles alone.

Life sucked.

So says the woman who owns a whole city block. That was a bit of an exaggeration, but my inner me had made its point. I had no business feeling sorry for myself.

"Wish me luck. I'm going in." I picked up my pace as I heard Joel softly call good luck after me. I walked by Ned and ignored his wink. I brushed past Jerry and ignored his glare. The silver-haired super duo was out in front, but between me and them was Michelle.

"Mind if I try giving the ball a throw?" I asked just as Michelle wrangled it from her dog's mouth. I tried to look pleased and not as if I wanted to wash my hands in a gallon of sanitizer when she put the saliva-slicked ball in my hand.

"Be sure to throw it away from traffic. Throw it into this upcoming yard."

My nerves instantly eased. Michelle's voice washed over me like that of a reassuring friend. Taking aim, I threw the ball and watched her dog go bounding after it. "Your dog is beautiful. What's his name?"

"Jessie." She bent down to pet him when he'd returned with the ball and managed to get the toy away from him again. "Who's my bestest pal? Who's my boy?" she cooed. He wiggled and whined his answer, soaking up every ounce of her attention and snapped playfully at the scarf that hung down from her neck. She threw the ball. "Go get it!" Jessie sprinted at lightning speed to fetch it.

"He really is a pretty dog," I said. I'd never been a dog person. Never been that much of a pet person despite the fact that I'd wanted one for years, but seeing their joy for each other made me envious.

"I saw you talking with Jerry." Her lips had gone from smiling to pinched.

Okay, no segue there. "He feels lucky to have you."

Her expression softened. "He's got some good stuff about him, too."

"But Rachel wasn't one of them?" If daggers could have shot out of her eye sockets, I'd have been dead.

"Rachel's in the past."

Really in the past, as in six-feet-under in the past. "Were you two friends?"

Michelle snorted. "No." She quickly amended. "Not enemies either, just not friends. She came on the walks just like the rest of us. She'd talk with Jerry sometimes, sometimes she'd talk to me. She'd bounce around."

I guessed that saying Rachel had "bounced around" was a polite way of saying what it was that she'd done. First she'd had an affair with Adam, then Jerry, then Ned. I'd seen basketballs with less *bounce*.

Jessie turned his happy attention to me, and I rubbed his ears. He really was a sweet dog.

We walked on a bit, letting Jessie be the

focus of our attention. Finally, Michelle filled the silence. "Rachel wasn't all bad. I felt sorry for her, to be honest. She was insecure, always trying to find ways to put other people down."

"She'd put you down?"

"Well, yeah, I'm people," she laughed, but it lacked mirth. We walked some more in silence before Michelle filled the void again. "I love Jessie so much." She gave the dog a hearty shoulder pat before throwing the ball for him again. "He means the world to me, so I know that having kids with Jerry is going to be amazing. He'll be a good dad and a good husband. It's what we want, and nothing Rachel had to say about it could change that."

"But she tried?"

"Sure she tried. She was always trying. She couldn't stand it when a man got away." She chuckled again, and this time there was mirth... malicious mirth. "Jerry stayed with me, and she couldn't *stand* that. She'd catch me in a private moment away from the others and say something like 'once a cheater, always a cheater.' And maybe she's right, but that doesn't take away the candlelit dinner he made for me the other night or the way he knows how to rub my feet when I've had a hard day. So he's not perfect. I'm not perfect." I watched her closely, wondering if she was saying what I thought she was saying. Had she strayed too? Is that why she'd been so willing to forgive Jerry for his wandering eye and roaming hands? Maybe she'd found some fun on the side, the same as him. "I'm just glad that sister of hers got the extra financial help that they needed." She got the ball from Jessie and threw it. "No matter what games Rachel was playing at, her sister was always nice to me, and she and her family have been really struggling. Now they're going to be okay. Rachel might not have been good for much in life, but she's done good for her sister in, you know…"

I did know. People had told me over and over and over, and I was starting to get the message.

Rachel was good and dead, good because she was dead.

CHAPTER 27

"The coffee's been made fresh and Melanie will be right out with the cookies," I said to the walking group members as they trundled past me into the café while I held the front door open. Their expressions ranged from friendly to mildly annoyed, but I didn't care. A stream of customers were walking into my café. Non-paying customers, but they were butts in seats, and that was a form of advertisement in and of itself for anyone who happened to walk by. An empty restaurant was a little like a dead animal lying on the side of the road: nobody wanted to get within ten feet of it.

As soon as the last one past by me, I jogged

over to Melanie. She was sitting at the grill's bar with her economics book out. She quickly put it away, though I didn't mind that she'd been studying. She was here, ready to help anyone who happened to walk in. That's all that mattered.

"Coffee, sugar, cream and a couple of plates of assorted cookies," I said, sounding slightly out of breath. It wasn't from the walking. It was from the excitement of having people in the café on a Saturday morning. I felt downright giddy.

"You got it, boss!"

I put together a tray of empty coffee cups and saucers, ready to go for when Melanie got ready for them. Then, I headed over to the cozy section and joined the group.

"Thanks for letting me bring Jessie inside," Michelle said. Her shoes were invisible with the dog laying directly on top of her feet. His head was down and his eyes were closed, peacefully resting.

"No problem." I didn't know if Jessie being in the café was a problem or not, but I wasn't about to call up the health inspector to find out. Thankfully I didn't see Sage in sight. Probably she was sleeping in some corner she'd picked out just for herself, and of course, I wasn't going to call the health inspector about her, either.

I took a spot in one of the overstuffed armchairs. Tucking my feet up under me, I settled back into the chair and let myself be lulled by the soft murmur of customers in my café. A smile found its way to my lips as I closed my eyes and let my ears' focus drift from person to person, picking up little snippets about their lives.

The retired couple's kids were going to visit next month, and that meant that they were going to get to see their grandbaby, Suzie.

Joel was talking with Adam about growing the newspaper's transition to becoming an online news service for the community. He hadn't figured out how to monetize it yet, but he had some ideas.

Jerry was trying to talk to Michelle, and she'd murmur a supportive word here or there, but he was having to do the heavy lifting in the conversation.

I opened one eye and glanced to the side of me at the sound of a chair being scooted closer. Ned sat down in it. "The place is lookin' nice. You've made some nice changes."

I hadn't made any changes, with the exception of chasing away all of the customers. "I appreciate you saying so." I decided to go with magnanimity over blatant honesty.

The door to the café jerked open and Dorothy—the bane of my existence—stormed in. Her hair was wild. Medusa wild. Her eyes were bulbous and made me seriously wonder at her sanity. "Get out!"

The shrill screech of her voice made me jump in my chair, and to my absolute astonishment Ned got up and stood between me and her, positioning himself like a shield. I had to lean to the side to see around him. No one else moved.

"Get out!" she screeched again, waving her arms in the same way a person would wade through water. It was as if she thought she could push everyone out of the café through her sheer force of will.

Still, no one moved and no one said a thing. Without anyone saying a word, Dorothy got the message. Everyone was staying put.

"Hell and damnation," she hissed, "that's what is coming to all of ya for canoodling with a murderess. Hell and damnation! 'Vengeance will be mine,' sayeth the Lord, and he will visit terrors untold upon all of your houses."

Silence followed. It would have been possible to hear a pin drop.

Dorothy didn't look well. A Y-shaped vein stood out prominently on her forehead, and her skin was a blotchy reddish purple.

"Dorothy," I said, "can Melanie get you a cup of coffee? Would you like to sit down? You could sit up at the grill counter. I wouldn't even come near, I promise." If she stroked out and died right in the middle of the café, I'd never be able to move past the reputation of being the place where people came to die.

Instead of answering, she narrowed her eyes and looked at Ned and then at me. "You always were a slut."

My mouth fell open, shocked. I'd only been with one man my entire life while Dan had slept with half the upper east side of Chicago. The nerve of her! I didn't get a chance to tell her what I thought of her, though, because she turned on her heel and headed back out the same way she'd come.

Ned sat back down, and nobody said a word. The walking group looked at each other and avoided looking at me.

Silver-haired wife then turned to silver-haired husband. "I think I'd like a bowl of spaghetti." Then to me, "I'd love to buy everyone a spaghetti brunch."

"Brunch is on us," the husband exclaimed, slapping the arm of his chair for emphasis.

My mouth fell open again, and then I smiled as tears filled my eyes.

I really was going to have to learn the names of that beautiful couple.

Joel leaned forward. "Let me know when you're ready for a write-up to go in the paper about the café and what you want it to say. I'll make it happen."

I felt my jaded little heart swell inside my chest.

The group's murmurs returned. People were talking. People were enjoying themselves.

I had a café with customers and a place within the community. I did my best to hide what I was doing as I swiped a tear away from my cheek.

I was home.

CHAPTER 28

*S*unday came with the whisper of a cold, chill wind blowing against my bedroom window. Fall was dying and winter was taking over.

Groaning, I rolled out of bed and dropped the few inches it took to reach the floor before climbing to my feet with a groan. Outside the sky was a deep gray and did not yet carry any of the warmth of the rising sun.

I put myself together and headed downstairs with Sage leading the way.

Brenda wasn't going to be in today. This was her one day of the week off. I wasn't expecting Sam in until after 10 AM. I had the place to myself, and I did with it the one thing I knew how to do. Clean. I mopped, I wiped and scrubbed, vacuumed and dusted.

I found Michelle's red and yellow striped scarf. It had gotten wedged between the cushions of the chair she had been sitting in.

The morning ticked on and Sam finally came. I made him and me a breakfast of under-cooked, runny oatmeal and burned toast. The jelly was good, though. It was from a jar I'd gotten at the store. Sam didn't complain.

I texted Zoey, told her about Michelle and the scarf and said I needed Michelle's address. She sent it back ten minutes later. I still hadn't told her about Max and swore I'd tell her one way or another before the end of the day.

By the time I left, Sam had his books out, the same as Melanie had done, and was studying at one of the tables. I didn't mind. I loved how enterprising and tenacious they both were. Neither of them had quit me or the café, and with no tips in sight, they both had plenty of reason to quit.

I gave my Uber driver the address, but we got lost twice on the way there. Finally, the car pulled up in front of a house matching Michelle's address and I got out. I'd meant for the driver to wait for me, but as soon as I was free of the car, he drove off. Frowning, I gave him a stern scowl and mentally gave him a one-fingered wave.

Michelle and Jerry's home was beautiful. It was small but everything about it was neat and tidy. The white house paint looked fresh, the green shutters were immaculate, and the walkway leading up to the front door was lined with some type of low-growing decorative plant with multicolored leaves.

I tried to open their fence's front gate but discovered it locked.

"They're not home," a disembodied woman's voice reached my ear. I looked around me for the source and spotted a forty-some-thing woman with long brown hair and natu-rally tanned skin across the street and one house down. "They're at church."

Sunday morning. Church.

I felt like a dope for not having thought of that possibility before I left the café. I didn't want to have to make a second trip to return Michelle's scarf, but I definitely wanted the kudos points for having made the effort. I needed every ounce of goodwill that I could garner.

I went across the street. "I was just returning

Michelle's scarf," I said, stopping at the edge of the woman's property as she headed over to meet me there. I held up the scarf as proof.

"Oh, she leaves that thing everywhere. I'll take it and give it to her."

I handed it over. "Hi, I'm Kylie Berry, the new owner of Sarah's Eatery."

Her eyes went wide. "You don't look anything like I'd imagined."

I stumbled on what to say to that. Ultimately, I didn't know if it was a compliment or an insult. "Thank you?" It came out sounding like a question, though I hadn't meant for it to. Wanting to move forward from the awkwardness, I quickly asked. "Have you lived here long?"

"I've lived in Camden Falls all my life. I'm Cindy Roberts."

Small town. Fish bowl. I took a shot. "It's nice to meet you. Did you by any chance know Rachel Summers?"

Cindy sucked in her breath and then *tsk*ed as she blew it out. "That poor girl, dying that way. I heard it was rat poison, same thing that happened to Michelle's dog a few months ago! And old man Matthews down at the end of the street was rushed off to the hospital two weeks after that. The family never would say what happened to him, but he'd been perfectly fine when I'd seen him the night before. He was old, but he ran marathons. There hadn't been anything wrong with him." She shook her head. "I don't know what gets into some people, but it's getting so that I don't feel safe leaving my door unlocked. This used to be such a quiet little place."

It wasn't quiet anymore? I glanced up and down the street. Other than Cindy and me, it was completely deserted. There wasn't even any traffic.

"Hopefully things will settle back down."

Cindy promised to give Michelle her scarf, and I texted for another Uber, hoping I didn't get the same driver who had dropped me off. While I walked slowly down the road away from the dead-end direction that Cindy had indicated, I thought about what she'd said. Michelle's dog had been poisoned, and the vet had said that Rachel had poisoned someone's dog.

It couldn't be a coincidence—it was such a small town. The vet had to have been talking about Michelle and Jerry's dog Jessie. On the walk he'd looked so good, so healthy. It never would have occurred to me in a million years that he'd gone through something as traumatic as being poisoned only a few months ago.

Maybe Rachel had been sorer about losing Jerry than Jerry had let on. If Rachel had been pulling femme fatale moves like poisoning his dog, there was no telling what she could have been capable of. Maybe whoever had poisoned her had thought that they were acting in preemptive self-defense.

CHAPTER 29

*J*t was Monday, mid-morning, and Brenda was already gone. There were a few customers in the café, but Melanie was taking café of them. I had no idea what she was serving them to eat.

"Is it supposed to look like that?" Zoey asked. Zoey was bent over and peering through the window of the oven at the from-scratch cake inside. I'd made it with Zoey standing by to verify that nothing hinky or life-threatening had gone into it. If someone keeled over while eating it, I didn't want anyone to be able to claim it was because something I'd done wrong. I was too cute to go to prison.

"What's wrong with how it looks?" I asked, bending down next to her to peer in.

"It's getting all golden around the edges but the center still looks wet and shiny. It's sunken in, too. What are those brown spots?"

"Raisins."

She looked at me.

"You saw me put them in."

"I was daydreaming."

"You're supposed to be my alibi if something goes wrong."

"Nobody's going to believe me. I'm almost as new in town as you. If you've been here less than two generations, you're a newcomer."

We both turned our attention back toward the cake.

"Is it a rum raisin cake, like the ice cream?"

"No…"

"Spice cake?"

"No."

"Did you follow a recipe?"

Pause.

She looked at me. "You didn't follow a recipe?"

I shrugged. "I followed a bunch of recipes! I picked out what I like and I like raisins."

We stood and Zoey crossed her arms over

her chest as her eyes scanned the room. Today she wore a vivid, brilliant blue eyeshadow above and below her eyes with a splash of hot pink in the center of her eyelid and the same hot pink as eyeliner on her lower lid. The outer corners were somehow swept up into a cat-eye shape. As for the rest of her, she wore a belted, light gray tunic dress that only reached a small way past her hips with midnight black high heel boots that came halfway up her thighs.

I was wearing a pair of jeans that were a week overdue to be washed and the t-shirt that I'd been sleeping in for nearly the whole time I'd lived here.

"I could install cameras to record what you do in here," Zoey said.

I looked at her warily.

She shrugged. "Closed circuit. I wouldn't spy!"

"You'd spy."

"Yeah, I would."

The timer went off and I got the cake out. The center sloshed and the edges were cracked like the Mojave Desert. "It'll be okay. I'll just put it back in and turn the temperature up." I put the cake in the oven and then stood up and stared at it. I had combined a lot of ingredients and then put them in the oven just like anybody else, and I couldn't understand why it wouldn't give me what I wanted back.

"You can't serve that," Zoey said. "Please don't serve that. I like you. I don't want you to go bankrupt and have to move away."

She had a point... I took a deep breath and blew it out. There was something else that we needed to talk about and I'd been avoiding it.

"Zoey, about Max—"

"You saw him, didn't you?"

"I did." I studied her face, looking for some sign of what she was feeling, but I couldn't get a read on her.

"My face recognition program has been pinging for days."

"What are you going to do? Have you spoken to him yet?"

"I'm going to feed him your brownies," she said, and I grimaced. "Sorry. Low blow."

"It's okay. I get it."

"I'm going to leave it alone for now... but that cake, that cake's gotta go, as in someplace other than this café and your customer's bellies. You can't serve that here."

She was right. "Any ideas what I should do with it?"

"There's a homeless shelter down past the railroad tracks."

"The homeless…" I looked again at the cake. The edges had gone from a golden color to something closer to a good sear on a steak. The homeless had so much to contend with already. I felt really guilty about the idea of giving them this cake. "Are you sure?"

"They're a tough and resourceful bunch. They'll figure out what to do with it."

That did make me feel better. "Okay."

We let the cake finish cooking so that the center no longer sloshed, and we wrapped it in tin foil. We both put on heavy coats and headed out on foot. The day was overcast and the clouds were having trouble making up their mind as to whether they wanted to snow or rain, so they were opting for something in between with a wet, frozen mist with minuscule snowflakes mixed in.

I followed Zoey's lead. We walked a ways, turned left, then a bit later turned right, walked some more, took a shortcut through the empty parking lot of a deserted drive-up restaurant and then hung another right. The cake was like a spongy brick tucked under my arm, and it was getting heavier by the second.

I glanced behind us for the third time. Each time I looked, no matter where we were in our journey, there was someone with a hoodie with their hands shoved deep in the jacket's front pockets. "Are we being followed?"

"I'm pretty sure. We could have been at the homeless shelter ten minutes ago, but I wanted to see if our tag along stayed with us."

I glanced behind us again. Whoever it was, was even closer. Their pace was definitely faster than ours now, and we were walking down a stretch of road that was devoid of houses, businesses or traffic. I did my best to picture Max and overlay his image with the person behind us. I was pretty sure it wasn't a match.

"What do you think we should do?" I asked. I was pretty sure that I could sprint for it, but Zoey's high heel boots looked to be at least four inches high. She wasn't having any trouble walking in them, but I wasn't sure how she'd do in a sprint.

"We stop." And that's just what we did. We stopped and turned as one.

The person following us slowed and eventually stopped about eight feet away. Their hood was pulled forward and their face was masked with shadow. Pulling one hand free from their pocket, the person brushed the hood back from their head to reveal wavy blonde hair with dark roots. Michelle smiled brightly. "Hi! What are you two up to?"

I blew out a breath of relief. "Michelle! What are you doing out here?"

"Getting a walk in. It helps me to think clearly."

I glanced around her. It was odd not seeing her frisky dog by her side. "Where's Jessie?"

"At home. Sometimes I like to just go out by myself."

I did not hear the ring of truth in her words; it was more like the gong of fibs.

Zoey stepped forward. "Why are you following us?"

"What are you talking about?" Michelle laughed, but it was thin and tinny. "I'm just out for a walk, the same as you."

"We're delivering a cake," I said, hoisting the offending pastry in front of me as proof of my words.

"You're the one on Kylie's fire escape looking in her apartment."

My mouth fell open and I saw her anew. The silhouette. The hoodie. It was her…

"Why were you spying on Kylie?" Zoey

demanded to know, and I held back the urge to point out who had the greater stalker tendencies between them.

"I wasn't!" Michelle was going from placating to indignant.

"Why did Rachel poison your dog, because it wasn't *Jerry's* dog she poisoned, was it? It was *your* dog. Jessie is *your* dog."

Michelle's expression went from placidly happy to an anguished mashup between rage and triumph. "He's *my* dog, and Rachel should have never come near him."

"So you killed her… you killed Rachel." It wasn't a question. There was no doubt.

Michelle's other hand withdrew from her hoodie jacket pocket, with a gun firmly in its grip. "You should have stayed out of my business."

"Somebody's gonna have to catch me up with what's going on," Zoey said, not sounding at all distressed about Michelle having a gun.

"Rachel had an affair with Michelle's husband, Jerry," I said, doing my best to at least appear to be as calm as Zoey seemed, although I was pretty sure she wasn't faking while I was completely faking.

"What's that got to do with their dog?"

"*My* dog!" Michelle snapped. "Jessie is *my* dog. He's always been my dog and he will always be my dog. That... that... that—"

"Jezebel? Harlot? Skank?" Zoey offered.

"Maybe we'd best just go with 'Rachel,'" I said, hoping not to use words to fuel Michelle's anger and thus get us killed in the crossfire of her rage, but hopes of that weren't looking good. Michelle was starting to wave the gun around whenever she spoke and she jabbed it forward like a pointing stick any time she wanted to emphasize a word.

"She tried to poison him! Jessie means the world to me and a good friend of mine was teasing me about it one day when Rachel was around. That's when it happened. I saw it in her eyes. She decided right then and there that she was going to hurt Jessie. Nooo, it wasn't enough that she was always trying to put me down, saying that I was fat or ugly or that my thighs were too heavy. She was always insinuating that everything not perfect about me was like a ticking time bomb for Jerry. Sooner or later he'd get tired of taking from the reject list and when he did, when he stopped feeling *sorry* or *obligated,* then he'd leave and she'd be right there. Ready and waiting."

"So this was about Jerry?" Zoey asked.

"NO! Aren't you listening? That... that... that...—"

Zoey said a string of words that made my ears burn. It started with the letter F and ended with the letter E.

"Yes! *That!*" Rachel exclaimed, jabbing the gun forward. "She came over to *my* house and poisoned *my* dog! I saw her sneaking off down the street and a few minutes later Jessie started vomiting and couldn't stop. Jerry's a grown man capable of making his own mistakes, but to touch my dog..." She shook her head. Her eyes were shining and tears were streaming down her cheeks.

"So you killed her," I said.

"I killed her. Didn't mean to, it's true. Thought she'd just get so sick she wished she were dead, but she had the good grace to go on and die. Only good thing she ever did."

"So the brownies weren't yours?" Zoey asked me.

"I told you they weren't mine!" I hissed back.

"Yeah, but you were wanted for murder. If I was wanted for murder, I'd say the brownies weren't mine, too."

"The brownies were mine!" Michelle screeched. "They were mine, okay. Have you seen her bake?"

I shifted the cake in front of me, feeling suddenly way more awkward. "I'm not that bad."

"You're pretty bad," Zoey said.

"You're bad," Michelle agreed.

"Okay, I'm bad," I said, rolling my eyes in annoyance.

"You really should take classes or something. I mean, how does someone even get that bad?" Michelle said.

"The brownies were from a mix!" I said in my own defense. "I followed the directions!"

"Yeah, and did those directions say to cook them until they were ready to be used as a brick to build a house? She would have broken her teeth on those things! I'd been baking goodies for Rachel for months, working up to the day that I'd poison her so that she wouldn't think me bringing her baked goods was weird. I wanted to make sure she'd eat them instead of throwing them away. When I went to her house that day and let myself into her backyard through the side gate, I was going to leave the brownies and then be on my way. She was always sunning herself back there, so I knew she'd get them. I never left them at her front door, and I didn't want to risk Nancy or her kids getting hold of the brownies and getting poisoned themselves. So, I went back there but she already had your brownies all laid out on a plate from the café."

"You swapped the brownies out, yours for mine?"

"Yeah, yeah," she said as she waved the gun around. "I didn't have anything against you, but you made it too easy—until you went and started snooping. Nobody would have done anything to you for accidentally killing her. Why couldn't you leave it alone?"

"You framed me for murder!"

"No, I framed you for being a terrible cook, which you are!"

"I can't take any more of this," I said to Zoey. That's when Zoey grabbed the cake out of my hands and flung it straight at Michelle's head like a high-speed frisbee. Michelle, screamed, shot at the cake and ducked all at the same time. I went into sprint mode and tackled Michelle in a flying leap. The gun went skittering across the asphalt, out of reach.

The cake had broken open next to Michelle's

head. "I am not a terrible cook!" I screamed as I scooped out a wad of the cake's undercooked center and shoved it in Michelle's face. "I do not kill people with my food!" I was holding my cake filled hand over her nose and mouth, making it impossible for Michelle to breathe. "I am not a danger to the community! I'm nice!" Michelle's hands were scrambling and her body was bucking.

In a rare moment of sanity, Zoey stepped in and pulled me off of her. "Let's try to make it so that the cops of someone other than you to arrest when they show up."

"Yeah, okay, okay. Yeah." My entire body was shaking. "Sounds good. Thanks, Zoey."

Zoey called the cops. I sat and stared at Michelle with both my hands filled with cake, ready to pounce on her if she made a move.

"You're nuts," Michelle said. Fear filled her eyes.

"I'm a divorcee who until recently was penniless and one day away from living on the streets. I'm doing just fine."

And I was.

$\mathcal{I}$ was in bed with Sage lying on top of me. She had her eyes half-lidded and rolled back in her head in utter bliss as I rubbed the side of her face. Suddenly, her eyes popped open and she lifted her head before using me as a springboard off of which to leap halfway to the open bedroom door. The soft glow of a light being turned on somewhere else in my apartment appeared a moment later.

Unless Sage had become profoundly adept at fending for herself or there was someone else in the apartment with me.

Getting up, I wrapped my blanket-dress around my waist, got one of my high heel shoes to use as a weapon and tiptoed to my door to peek out. Brad was standing near the front door, facing the kitchen, and there were a couple of bags at his feet. He was unbuttoning and rolling up the sleeves of his officer's uniform. I could have stood there watching him all night. He was poetry in motion.

"Get yourself out here," Brad called without even looking my way. He then disappeared out of view and into the kitchen.

Sighing heavily, I drooped my head and considered my options. I could get completely dressed, fuss my hair, sneak across the hall to the bathroom and brush my teeth and put a light dusting of makeup on before going out to talk to the man who had just broken into my apartment in the middle of the night, or I could go as is and he would simply have to deal with the reality that was me.

I opted for reality. I didn't dress. I did nothing to smooth my bed hair, and I kept my high heel weapon in my hand.

I padded down the hallway in my bare feet until Brad came into view. He was in the kitchen washing his hands.

"What are you doing here?"

"Eggs," he said. "They're one of the easiest foods to cook and one of the hardest ones to master." He turned off the water, dried his hands on a paper towel, and then lifted a bag onto the counter. Out of it he took out three one-dozen cartons of eggs. "Do you have a frying pan?"

"No."

He reached down and picked up a second bag, out of it he took out some butter, a couple of frying pans and a couple of spatulas. "You do now."

"Brad, what are you doing here?"

"You shouldn't have done that today."

"Done what?"

"Put yourself in danger." He locked my eyes with his, and they were filled with incrimination. "Some of us would care if something happened to you."

My heart tripped over itself.

"So, you've got over easy eggs, over medium, over hard, sunny side up, poached, hard boiled, soft boiled, soft scrambled, hard scrambled, omelets, frittatas, baked, and scotch eggs."

He was giving me a cooking lesson. "Why are you doing this?"

"You know why I'm doing this," he said, but he'd dropped his gaze to focus on the items he'd brought, and I believed that he was purposefully not looking at me.

"No, I don't."

He lifted his brilliantly blue gaze to meet mine, and this time my heart forgot to beat. "I want you to stay, but to stay, you've got to get better at stuff like this." He waved at all the raw eggs.

Brad Calderos cared about me. He cared what happened to me and he cared about where and how I lived my life. I was smiling from ear to ear. I wasn't even going to ask for my key back this time.

"How do you like your eggs?" I asked.

"Oh, that's easy. Poached. But that's a pretty advanced technique. We should save it for another night."

Butterflies took flight within me and tickled all my senses, but then I remembered the whole being under suspicion for murder. "Less than twelve hours ago you thought that I'd killed Rachel."

"You didn't kill Rachel."

"You know that *now*." I joined him in the kitchen and took up a spot beside him.

"I knew that before. I knew it always."

"How?"

"You can't cook. No one would have eaten your brownies." In a sly move that happened so fast that I didn't even have time to think about it, he kissed me on the forehead and then turned his attention to the stove.

"I can cook!" It was such a lie. I didn't know why I was saying it. It was so harsh to hear everyone around me tell me over and over again that I couldn't cook.

"You are the worst cook I have ever met in my life. Ever. Men and women included. Men who have never stepped in a kitchen before. You're the worst." He clicked one of the burner flames to life, turned the setting to low and put one of the frying pans on top of it before cutting a dab of butter and dropping it in. "I have never seen anyone with so little natural talent for it. You should work to master a few small dishes and hire a chef for everything else."

"I'm not that bad!"

"You are."

"I'm not, and I'll prove it."

He stopped mid-egg crack, holding the shell encased egg over the sizzling pan. "How?"

"By doing all the cooking myself. All of it. No chef."

"Not even Brenda?"

I faltered. "Well, I gotta have some time out of the kitchen sooner or later."

He smirked and my palms itched for cake to rub in his face.

"Move over." I pushed him out of the way and took over the frying pan. The butter was bubbling and I didn't know what to do next. "What do I do?"

His large, solid form moved behind me, and my cheeks pinked for reasons having nothing to do with the stove's heat. I definitely hadn't thought things through. "First, you break an egg." He demonstrated by cracking and opening the egg with one hand. "Your turn." He put an egg in my hand. I hit it against the side of the pan and the egg's shell shattered, sending white and yellow goo everywhere.

Brad chuckled in my ear, giving me goosebumps all over. "Like I said, worst cook ever."

"Today," I agreed, "but, you know, maybe not next week."

"You're right. Maybe…"

CHAPTER 31

The next morning, Joel, Agatha, Zoey, Jack, and Brad lined the stools of my bar's grill as I served up each one of them an omelet loaded with their choice of toppings. Joel's omelet was stuffed with sharp cheddar cheese and diced tomatoes. Agatha's omelet was filled with crumbled bacon and feta cheese. Zoey's was zucchini, feta, mushrooms and bacon. And Brad's was stuffed with mushrooms, Colby, diced sweet onion, and bacon.

Everyone was digging in and everyone had smiles on their faces, including me.

"This is amazing," Joel said. "When did you learn how to do this?"

I eyed Brad and blushed but kept his

nocturnal cooking lesson to myself. "I've been practicing."

"Have you decided what I want to say about the café in a write-up?"

I slowly nodded my head, suddenly not feeling as sure about my decision. "Yes. I want it to say that all meals will be personally prepared by the café's owner, Kylie Berry."

Everyone stopped eating—everyone that is except for Brad. He'd heard these plans last night. Now he simply smiled while shaking his head, but he didn't stop eating.

Agatha was the first to speak. "Sweetheart, you're an absolute dear, but are you sure you want to do that?"

I shook my head no, but then said, "Yes."

Jack chuckled deep and low, coal-dark eyes sparkling. "Brave girl. This is to you." He raised a piece of his omelet in salute before devouring it in one bite.

"I also want the article to say that I'll have an Oops board, and anything that doesn't turn out well will go up on that Oops board to be sold at a steep discount."

"Smart. That should help to create some curiosity and some buzz," Joel said.

"Not to mention bring in some penny pinchers," Zoey added. "The college crowd or people operating on a tight budget will love it."

I smiled, happy to have my ideas embraced rather than shot down. I'd been so nervous about naming myself the sole cook that I'd tossed and turned half the night.

"What kinds of foods will you offer?" Joel asked.

"I'll keep it simple. Today is all about omelets. Tomorrow…" I shrugged. I'd have to give that some more thought.

"Will there be any more murder hunting in your future?" Jack asked.

"No," Brad answered at the same time that Joel said, "That'd be a great hook!"

They looked at each other, and I could have sworn that I saw them glare.

"No more murders," Brad said. "This is a quiet, sleepy town. We have our issues, but murder's not one of them. Our little Kylie will just have to be satisfied with the boring, everyday life of a downtown Camden Falls property and business owner."

"And murder solver extraordinaire!" I said, clapping my hands together. "Put that in there too, Joel."

Brad choked but Joel laughed. "Sure thing.

Anything for you. You want to include anything else?"

I looked over at the glass front door where I could see the scrawled, backward name of Sarah's Eatery. "Tell them that the café's name is changing, too." There was a chorus of *ohhh*s as people turned to look at the café door and then at me.

"What will you name it?" Zoey asked.

I smiled and felt a warmness grow around my heart. "The Berry Home."

JOIN THE AR WINTERS NEWSLETTER!

Find out about the latest releases by AR Winters, and get access to exclusive free copies of her books:

Click Here To Join

You can also follow AR Winters on Facebook

Made in United States
North Haven, CT
01 April 2025

67470911R00148